THE CORE

Alice

Nola Sarina & Emily Faith

1

Table of Contents

Where I Belong

This place is my life.

The Core. The place that *saved* my life.

Everyone here looks at me like a queen: the goddess of the dance floor, matchmaker extraordinaire. And I've earned the title, dancing my heart out four nights a week, picking up on who will fit well with whom... sometimes for just a night. Sometimes for life.

I'm not being braggy, I swear. It's happened. Les and Greg got married last week, and Tony and Sarah are having a baby soon. A *planned* baby. None of those no-condom whoopsies go down when I'm in charge.

The music pulses through me like life itself. Go-go dancers are wild in their cages above the dance floor, illuminated by strobe lights and a disco ball. I wave at one of the girls up there, and she blows me a big, affectionate kiss. The booths along the wall aren't full, but they're close... many couples enjoying private drinks and getting cozy in the most intimate ways under the shadows. The flashing lights glint off the sequins of my dress, and I silently compliment myself on the choice of silver and black. I chuckle quietly. I kind of match the chrome and black leather décor of The Core, while Andee looks more like the neon-painted graffiti wall.

My best friend is spinning through the dance floor with two glasses of champagne in her hands. God, the way she dances is hypnotic. She's learned so much since she started working here six months ago, and she's so comfortable with people that some nights she out-matchmakerizes *me*. The couple she hands the glasses to—discreetly passing the gentleman a condom, as I taught her to do out of the eyesight of the woman—look like they might just make it for the long haul. Andee's perception of compatibility is as sharp as mine, and I'm *so* damn proud of her. She's come a long way since she walked into this club sheepish and afraid to show her true self.

I can tell what everyone around me needs. I can sense when a guy hasn't had a proper blow job in years, or when a girl hasn't had a guy make her come in her life. It's just something I detect when I talk to them, by the way they move their hands, fidget, or avoid eye contact. A girl who's squirming in her seat is often so deprived of orgasms I know I have to pair her up with one of the best in the club. Chris, maybe. Or Shaun. Hell, I've resorted to pulling in favors from Derek when a girl *really* needs to get off, or is hesitant to do so. That's how Andee looked when she got here, and now she's a goddess of this place, too. I just *know* these things. I'm never wrong.

A throat clears behind me. I turn on my bar stool and meet the warmest pair of green eyes I've ever seen. It takes me a minute to look beyond them at the guy wearing them: he's blonde, tall, and wearing a black button-down shirt over washed-out jeans. *God,* he's gorgeous. He stands beside me, leaning his elbow coolly on the bar, looking from my eyes to my lips and back up again.

"Hi," he says.

"Sorry," I manage, laughing nervously as I slide off my barstool. Why the hell am I nervous? "I didn't see you come in. I'm Alice."

He shakes my hand. "Evan. Derek invited me."

One of the boss's recruits. Better make sure he's *really* satisfied. I'm aiming for a promotion, after all. "Oh, wow. Where did you meet him?"

Evan shrugs, and I notice for the first time how thickly muscled his shoulders are. "I work on his truck from time to time. Put in the new lift kit a couple weeks ago."

A mechanic. Good with his hands, then, and strong... probably able to go for quite a long time. But also a hard worker who needs someone enthusiastic. He needs a girl who wants it *bad.* I glance over my shoulder. A girl with long, blonde curls is dancing with her girlfriends by the DJ booth, and I pegged her when she walked in as needing a thorough, full-body fuck. Somebody who appreciates her as much as she appreciates him, not just a quick poke. They'll match up well.

I shoot Evan a sneaky grin. "I know what you want."

He lifts his eyebrows and takes a sip of the bourbon sloshing around ice cubes in his glass. "Do you?"

I nod, taking his hand. "Come on. I'll show you."

Evan doesn't let me pull him away from the bar. He clasps my hand and tugs until I crash against his chest with a grunt. "Whoa," I say.

"Alice."

His breath his sweet, and I peer up into those startling greens. I'm right against his chest. He could hammer nails with his pecs.

He lets a grin play on the edges of his lips and brushes a strand of my dark hair back from my eyes. I crane up, inches from his lips. "Yes, Evan?"

"What if I've already seen what I want?"

And then his lips are on mine.

What The Hell Is Happening?

Evan kisses me gently at first, just the try-out kiss, his lips closed around mine. My breath catches and I struggle to form a thought. What do I do? No one just *kisses* me. I'm in charge of this shit.

He holds there for a moment, and then releases his breath with a groan and slides his hand around my lower back, pulling me against him. Oh, that sound. It's deep, loaded with desire and entirely for *me*.

Shit! I can't let this happen. No strings attached, here. No strings allowed, and the way his groan punches me straight in the heart is not okay. Punch me in my panties? Sure. But anything else could mean we're connecting, and I'm not about to set *that* kind of example for Andee or anyone else here. The few couples who have made it for the long-haul after meeting in The Core are the exception, not the expectation.

I break the kiss, putting a hand on his chest and push him back an inch. *Who has pecs like this, seriously?* When he releases my lips, he's grinning brightly, his eyes even more captivating when he looks this happy. I want to scold him for the kiss, but I can't stop grinning right back at him.

"What was that?" I ask.

Evan shrugs. "A kiss? I think it was a kiss." He smirks.

"Of course it was a kiss," I say. "But why? You're not here for me."

"I'm not?" He cocks an eyebrow up.

Gah, I'm trying to be irritated with him and he just gets cuter every minute that goes by. I laugh. "No, you're not. You're here to meet someone special, aren't you?"

Evan slides his fingers off my waist and stuffs both hands in his pockets. I savor a moment of private despair as he stops touching me. But this is my job: I match them up. I make them happy. If it means I sacrifice a few intimate options in the process, then so be it. I'm gunning hard for that promotion. Andee doesn't need me on the floor anymore, and I can still help her if I manage the place.

Evan sighs, peering into my eyes. He could stop traffic with them, they're so piercing. "Yeah, I'm here to meet someone special. I thought I just did."

My heart sinks. Why, I don't know. I let out a sigh and look away from those eyes, afraid they'll sway me into another kiss if I stare any longer. "Sorry, Evan," I say, my voice harder than usual. "I'm not part of the deal."

"Deal?"

"Didn't Derek tell you about this place?"

"Yeah, he said The Core is a club where anything goes. No rules, and nobody gets hurt."

"And I'm in charge of it." I wink. "I'm a matchmaker here, and I get to pair you up with someone who wants the same thing as you do."

Evan looks around. "That doesn't make any sense."

"Why not?"

He shrugs. "Because you're off-limits? That's stupid."

I glare at him. "It's not stupid."

"Yeah, it is. You want the same thing I do, right?" He cocks an eyebrow, and I have to look away. I don't have an answer for that. "Why can't you get what you want, too?" Evan finishes.

"Well... I can." Andee's first night—in the elevator with Isaiah and Jude—flashes into my memory, and I shake it away, not needing an extra arousal as I'm standing next to this Greco-ideal man. "Just not tonight."

"Why not?"

I let out an exasperated sigh. Evan is friends with the boss. I can't let him know I'm aiming for a better job. I don't want to come across as ungrateful to Derek for all he's done for me, I'm just... ready for more.

"Just because, okay? Now come on." I take his hand and tug him out onto the dance floor.

Doing My Job

Evan follows me, his hand in mine. He runs his thumb over my knuckle, his skin a bit rough, and I ignore the way I clench inside at his touch. His hands are big, strong. Just the way I like them. I shake the thought off and focus on the music. The beat draws me away from that nagging longing, brightening my mood.

We hit the dance floor and I break into motion automatically, pulling Evan as I do. He doesn't dance, just walks with me, watching every move I make. This is so natural for me. I love moving this way, letting the music decide what my body does. The DJ is on fire tonight, the pace of the dancers manic. I toss my hair out of my eyes—I'm loving the new extensions I had put in last week, making my dark hair cascade almost down to my waist—and throw my arms around Evan's neck, dancing along his body. Fuck me, he's solid. And tall. Like, over six feet. Damn.

I stretch up to his ear as his hands find my lower back again. "Everyone wants something different," I say, "and my specialty is knowing what they want. Can you trust me?"

His breath is harsh against my cheek. "Yes. I trust you."

I slide a condom into his palm. "Then *really* trust me. Go with it. I won't steer you wrong."

Evan fingers the condom for a moment, and then pulls back to search my eyes, his brow furrowed. I kiss his cheek gently, and then pull him further into the crowd.

We reach the booths behind the dance floor and I scoot into one where Curly Blond sits with her friends, two drinks in and totally having a blast. "Hey!" I say.

"Hi," Curly Blond says, eyeing up Evan with her jaw slightly dropped. "You're Alice, right?"

Of course I am. I nod and give her an excited grin. "So, I was thinking. This isn't your first time here, is it?"

Curly Blond shakes her head. "No, I was here once with Christopher." Her eyes fog over for a moment: she must be remembering the night Andee paired her up with the rich, rough-fucking sex God.

"Evan here is looking for someone to hang out with for a little bit. Mind keeping him company?"

Curly Blond gazes up at Evan and then scans down his body with her eyes. She lets out a quiet laugh. "Uh, yeah. I think I can do that."

Evan shifts as we check him out together. I scoot out of the booth and lean to him. "Have fun, okay? Find me after."

He shoots me a perplexed look as I dance off into the crowd, Curly Blond rising to take my place.

He'll like her. I know he will. She's in desperate need of someone who makes her feel as important as she does for him. And he's so fucking sexy, there's no way she'll do it half-assed. He needs a girl with enthusiasm. I don't look over my shoulder to see if they start dancing or kissing. It's not my job to watch, just my job to make sure they hit it off and get it on.

I try not to think about the nagging pang in my heart that I just took someone I *really* wanted to taste and handed him off to someone else. She'll be good to him, though. *She'd better.*

I wander back to the bar. Andee's got most of the dance floor under control... I don't see any singles anywhere. Everyone's paired up. A smile warms my face... seeing The Core running at its intended pace makes me happy. Everything here makes me happy. It's been home for so long. I rap on the bar and the bartender slides me a cold Sprite. I drink with Andee some nights, but we're busy enough tonight I should probably stay off the sauce in case she needs help with anything.

"My ears are ringing," Andee says, sliding up into the barstool next to me, sweaty and gorgeous as always.

I chuckle and face her. "Must have heard me thinking about you!"

She narrows her eyes at me. "Am I doing something wrong?"

I nudge her with my shoulder. "You always assume that, but no. Never. I was just thinking about what an excellent job you're doing. You're so on-the-ball I'm almost bored."

"You didn't *look* bored when you were dancing with that tall drink of lick-ableness." Andee smirks, dragging her hand through her long hair and shaking it out behind her.

"Evan? Yeah, I paired him up with Curly Blond over there."

"Seriously, Alice? You're way too generous. I woulda kept that one for myself."

"Want me to see if he's up for round two when he's done?"

Andee grins. "Sure. Why not?"

Andee and Evan will have fun together. Definitely. She's always up for anything, and she fucks like a champ. I shake off that obnoxious pang of longing and take another pull on my Sprite as the music shifts.

"Oh my God!" Andee squeals. "Do you know what song this is?"

I shake my head. "DJ hasn't played it in a while, has he?"

Andee grabs my hand. "This is the first song we danced to on my first night here. Remember?"

Is it really? I don't remember. That night was so incredible the last thing I'd remember about it is the music. But the beat is heady, alluring, so when she tugs me off my stool and into the crowd, I follow happily.

We dance around each other, on each other. It's erotic, and those around us watch. Taking us in as we move, hips in rhythm, bodies pressed together. Andee's bare leg slips between mine, and I dance along her, dragging my hand over her thigh. The touch of her always lights me up. She's so open, so free. She throws her head back and shimmies as she dances, and we just don't stop. We dance through the end of the song and beyond, moving without thought. This is my happiness. This is my release.

Andee stops dancing as suddenly as we started, her expression something serious and surprised. I stop too, puzzled, and follow her gaze behind me.

At the end of the dance floor stands Evan, his arms crossed over his chest. He looks angry. Furious, even. *Oh, no.* I haven't screwed up a pairing yet. He must not have liked Curly Blond.

"Go figure out what happened," Andee urges me.

I shoot her an apologetic smile and cross the dance floor to Evan.

"What's up?" I say, my heart pounding even harder than the beat of the music. I hate being wrong, and the thought that I might have angered a customer—a friend of the boss, no less—sends a clawing fear into my stomach.

"Can I talk to you?" Evan says. "Privately."

13

Oh, shit. "Sure," I say. "Booth okay?"

He nods, his green eyes hard, and I glance around for Curly Blond. "Where's your date?"

"She's not my date."

She's not? Did they fuck already? She didn't go home upset, did she? We never have that kind of drama at The Core. Ever. Shit, I really messed this one up. My mind reels and I twist my fingers together in front of me as I walk, trying to calm my nerves.

I lead Evan to a booth and slide into it. He sits beside me, moving close. Too close. My heart pounds harder as I draw in a breath of his cologne. He doesn't look sweaty, no just-fucked fog in his eyes.

I can't take the suspense anymore. "What happened, Evan?"

"I tell you I'm interested in *you*, and you send me off to fuck someone else? How screwed up is that, Alice?"

Screwed up? "It's my job. What happened? I need to know these things. Fill me in. If something went wrong, I need to fix it." I'm rambling... a product of my erratic nerves.

"She's fine," Evan snaps. "She's with her friends and she's happy."

O....kay. "Why are you angry? You two had fun, right?"

"We had fun for the whole ten minutes we spent talking." Evan slaps the condom down on the table, unopened.

I blink at it, surprised. "If you're not into it, it's cool. Whatever you're into I can make happen." God knows I've seen enough of this place to know that unique sexual preferences call for special handling, sometimes.

"It's not that, Alice."

"Evan, I don't judge," I say. "I've paired up more men with men and men with couples than you can imagine. Whatever you're into goes. You wanna wear high heels or lick whipped cream off enormous tits, it's cool. I can make it happen."

He groans. "I am *not* into that stuff. Stephanie was fine. It wasn't her, it was me. She understands that." He points across the dance floor and I lean across him to see her curly blond hair bouncing as she laughs with her friends by the bar.

"What's wrong, then?" I ask. I return my gaze to Evan. I'm sitting closer to him than I expected, and his breath rushes across my face. *Whoa.*

He takes my chin in his fingertips. He licks his lips to speak, and when he does, his voice is softer. "What's wrong is that you're not listening to me. I've already seen what I want. I've already told you."

I try to pull away, but he just leans closer, forcing me to stare into his eyes. God, they're green. Enchanting. Even in the darkness of the club I can see so many layers to them. "You don't want me," I manage.

"Why wouldn't I?"

There are so many reasons. Shit I don't want to delve into with him. The less he knows about me—about my history—the better. Andee is the only one here besides Derek who knows it all. "You can have anyone here. I can make it happen. Just tell me who."

"Okay," Evan says, and he kisses me again.

This time, his kiss is gentle, pleading. He's asking me to let him kiss me. He's begging me not to pull away.

I should pull away. This isn't part of my job. Even the fun I had on Andee's first night was different because I wasn't emotionally invested in it.

Is that why I'm so resistant to fooling around with Evan? Do I *like* him, like more than just a fuck? The rule in The Core is no-strings-attached. If I like him more than just as a one-night-stand, I'm obligated to say no.

15

Evan parts his lips just a little bit, letting his tongue flick over my lower lip, and I moan, climbing astride his lap. He threads his fingers into my hair and kisses me deep, letting his mouth wander down my neck. He groans, and exhales the word, "Yes..."

I don't think. I just move, allowing the music to tell me where to go and what to do. I roll my hips against him and his breath rushes out. "Alice," he says.

"Yes, Evan?" I can hardly form the words as the tip of his tongue drags along the line of my chin and he crushes my lips again.

"I want you," he says. "Please." His hands tighten around my waist as he asks.

I know better than this. I know *way* better than this. But his body between my legs feels so fucking good. I slap my hand down on the table behind me, grabbing the condom.

"Okay," I say, sliding it back into his palm.

Okay. I Want It.

Evan doesn't hesitate. He seizes my lips with his, letting his tongue sweep over mine once. I moan at the taste. He's delicious, and my hands wander over him without conscious thought. I can't get enough of the feel of his pecs, his shoulders. He's built fucking solid, his hands are warm and firm on me, possessive. Fire ignites in my core and spreads down between my legs. I want him.

He shifts me up to sit on the table, his hands dragging over my thighs as he slides my glittery dress up to expose more skin. I moan, taking in the sight of his body. I wonder what his chest looks like beneath his shirt, and I reach forward to tug it up, but he stops me with a firm hand on my wrist.

"Not here," he says.

I forget, sometimes, that I might be cool with stripping down to nothing in the middle of The Core, but others might be a bit shyer about taking off their clothes. I let a smile play across my lips and whisper an apology. Moving so the view of him is blocked by my body, I reach down to his belt and pull it open.

He doesn't need any further permission than that. He flips open the button of his jeans and springs free, his erection thick and long. *Yes.* I want this. I want him.

Evan rolls the condom on. "You ready for me?"

Good God, yes, I'm ready. I move off the table and straddle his lap, pulling my panties to the side with one hand beneath my skirt. I'm wet, and as he sinks into me, he strokes along just the right spot and I suck in a gasp.

Evan waits until I'm settled all the way around him, and then he kisses me again, a slow pull on my lips. "Is this okay?" he asks, his breath rushing along my skin.

"Yes," I whisper. "God, yes."

"Then move, baby," he says.

The music does it for me. I move in rhythm with it, lifting and settling along his length. He fits me just right, his thickness rubbing that perfect spot. I lose my breath quickly, overwhelmed by the sensations of his length inside me, so Evan pulls my face to rest against his shoulder as he takes over. He grabs onto my hips and lifts me, rocking into me. I close my eyes, whimpering. He feels so fucking good. A rush of pleasure floods through me as he digs his fingers into my hips, holding me tight. Possessing me. I can't think.

Evan fucks me harder, and I move with him... bucking against his hardness, begging for more of him inside me. He's so long. So thick. My wetness coats him, and I can't even help the way I cry out every time he buries it inside. Sweat breaks out on my lower back, and Evan presses up hard into me, filling me. I shriek at the intensity of it, but he presses harder still. The music drowns out my moans.

He wraps his arms around me and crushes me to his chest, buried inside my wetness. He moves slowly, sliding all the way out and pushing back in, and his muscles against my body flex and thicken with the motion. I grab his chest, trail my hand over his abs... he's perfect. Delicious. I open my mouth to taste the skin of his neck as he slides in and out, breathing more harshly with every thrust. A five o'clock shadow scratches against my cheek, and this combination of rough and yet soft

18

with him is erotic as hell. When I slide my tongue up the side of his neck to his earlobe and bite it, he growls and picks up his pace.

I straighten, pressing my forehead to his. He kisses me, breathless, and fucks me harder. I moan into his mouth and then break the kiss, gasping as we move with each other. His eyes are so intense, blazing green fire. It's too much. Too intense. He slides quicker in and out of me, and the intensity builds in my core.

I tear my eyes away from his. I can't look at him. He rolls me down to lay in the dark booth, and I throw my arm over my face, covering my eyes. He fucks me harder still, pounding in and out of me, every thrust earning a shriek from my lips. It builds on and on, the pleasure surging through me. He kisses my neck, his hand wandering up to pinch my nipple through my shirt, and the touch is so electric I lose it. I burst at the seams, arching my back off the seat, bucking my hips and coming around his hardness.

Evan groans, "Oh, yes," with every spasm of my wetness around him. His body is so hard against me, and the orgasm ricochets from my toes to my head, quivering, crying out as he rocks me on and on. He buries his face in the crook of my neck. "Alice. Yes, baby, come on me."

I can't stop coming. He's too gorgeous, too sexy, and I cry out again as a second orgasm rips over me, unexpected and sudden. He growls against my neck and pounds in time with the spasms of my body.

And then he slams it into me one final time, stroking right along that spot, and reaches his climax. He groans as he releases inside me, breathless, and I'm so tender, so sensitive, that I jump with every throb. Evan's breath is hot and harsh against my neck, and I turn to reach his lips. Kissing him deeply, I close my eyes, letting him worship my mouth with his.

More To It Than That

Evan recovers slowly, kissing me the whole time. "Alice," he whispers. "You're so fucking perfect."

My eyes fly open with alarm. Perfect? Shit. He's getting attached already.

I try to diffuse the mood. "You're not so bad yourself," I say with a wink.

He pulls back to study my eyes for a moment, and then withdraws from me with a clear of his throat. I gasp as he pulls out, still so sensitive from not one, but *two* orgasms. I haven't had a double in I-don't-know-*how*-long.

I sit up and adjust my skirt, running a hand through my hair to make sure it's all in place. I'll have to stop back at my changing room anyway and clean up before I continue with the night anyway. Damn. Evan fucked me good.

"Not so bad?" he says as he zips up his fly.

I catch a hint of worry in his tone. "Okay, you were great," I say with a laugh.

Evan grins at me. God, that smile. I let out a giggle, and then put a hand to my mouth to stop myself. Am I giggling? Evan makes me giggle?

I can't giggle. I can't get all girly, all nervous, all anything. I'm in charge here, dammit. It's just sex. I wish he'd lay off the compliments so I'd stop acting like a swooning schoolgirl.

Evan blows out his breath in a rush. "Well. This has been an interesting night, to say the least."

"All nights are like this, here," I say. "It's what we do."

"So if I come back tomorrow night... we can do this again?"

"Not with me," I'm quick to say. "But maybe tomorrow night you'll let me do my damn job."

His grin falls. "Your job."

"Yeah. I mean, I don't mind doing the intro-fuck for some people. And believe me, Evan, you were worth it. I don't often come twice during sex."

"Bet I can make you come four times."

My jaw drops. "What?"

He shrugs, that grin back on his face. "I like a challenge."

Good God, four times? YES. "Evan, you have the wrong idea."

A frown creases his forehead. "I have what wrong idea?"

I shake my head, putting a few inches of space between us. "About this. Me. Like I said, I don't mind an intro-fuck, but you can't come back here for me. You have to come back here for you, to explore new things."

"I thought this place was anything-goes."

"It is. That's exactly my point."

He drags a hand through his hair, frustrated. "And I get to have whatever I want?"

I know where this is going. "You can't just decide you want *me* and keep coming back for me. I have a job to do." Speaking of... *shit*. I've left Andee on her own for far too long,

22

and Derek will probably be on the floor soon. I'm not earning my promotion by fucking in a booth.

Evan takes my hand and pulls it to his lips. He kisses my fingertips gently, and I'm lost in the intensity of his eyes. "Alice," he says.

God, I melt whenever he says my name.

"If I can't come back here for you, I'd like to take you out sometime. Dinner, maybe. Drinks. I'll take up that four-time challenge after." He cracks a wry smile.

He's asking me out. My heart pounds, and I can't form a sentence. I haven't been asked out in years. He doesn't just want to fuck me. He wants to *date* me, to get to know me. To talk. I haven't talked to anyone in so long other than Andee. She knows it all... my old, bad habits and the way they still haunt me every now and then. She knows about my family and how angry I am at them, still.

Maybe Evan will just take me out once, fuck me, and get it over with.

Or maybe he deserves someone better than damaged goods who wants to *get it over with.* He definitely deserves someone who won't disappoint him at every turn.

I can't do this. But he keeps stroking his thumb over my knuckles, and I'm lost in his gaze... I don't know how to tell him no. He's strong, delicious, and a fucking amazing lover. He fits me just right inside, and his hand clasped around mine fits, too. He's everything I've ever wanted in a man, but everything I know I'd just lose eventually if I had. I always screw good things up.

"Alice!" Derek's voice booms from the back of the booth row.

I jump and scoot past Evan, climbing right over his lap to get out of the booth.

"Derek," I say to the boss, ruffling my hair again as I stride over to him. I put on my best walk of confidence as I approach, smiling at him. He's one person I respect a hell of a lot. He introduced me to a life I never imagined when I showed up here, and guided me to a better place of acceptance with myself. I drink in the sight of his dark arms, his tattooed bicep. Admiring his physique reminds me of Evan's hard-as-rock abs, and I clench deep down inside. *Twice.* He really made me come twice.

Derek smirks at me, and I feel my skin flush, hoping he didn't see too much of Evan and me. He doesn't mind when I recreate during my shift occasionally, but he doesn't like me too distracted on the job during busy nights, either.

"What's up, boss?" I ask.

"Andee's with a couple of nervous gentlemen. Would you mind taking care of the small birthday party we've got coming in? Four ladies. They should show up any minute."

I glance around the bar. Andee's by the edge of the dance floor, trying to break the ice between two guys who look like they want each other, but don't know how to close those last few inches and touch. I grin as she laughs with them, diffusing tension. She'll handle it.

"Do we even have enough singles for that?" I ask Derek. "Everyone's pretty paired up tonight." The last thing we need is a reputation for being a couples-only venue. A birthday party with no men to join the fun. *That* would be a buzz-kill.

He shrugs. "I asked a few buddies to come in tonight... they know the rules. I see you've already met Evan."

I flush even hotter. "Yes, I met Evan."

"So introduce him to the girls," Derek says, and I keep my poker face on.

"You got it!"

He narrows his eyes. "Unless, of course, you're not okay with that, Alice."

"Why wouldn't I be okay with it? It's what I'm best at."

He leans closer and murmurs, "Because you looked awfully comfortable over there."

I pull back and avert my gaze. Busted.

"I'm not mad," Derek says with a chuckle. "You like him. He's a decent guy."

I force a laugh. "Like him? Nah. He was fun, but that's it. I'll get him passed off to the next pair of wet panties I find."

Derek cringes as I speak so loudly, and then gazes over my shoulder.

I peer back and am met by those green eyes. Evan. Shit, he heard me.

He scoffs and shakes his head, turning to leave. I'd admire his immaculately sculpted back, but he's walking away from me, totally offended.

"Evan, wait," I call before I even think.

He faces me and spears me with his glare. "Wait for what? I get it. You're not interested. I guess I should have listened the first time."

The hurt in his voice is so plain. He asked me out and I replied by treating him like a doormat, passing him around for the next set of dirty boots that wants to stomp all over him. Or wet panties, in this case.

"It's not that," I say, my voice shaking. Now that he's pulling away, I want him so bad I can hardly see. I want to say *yes* to him. I want to see him again, to fuck him again, to maybe even talk with him.

"Forget it," Evan says. "It doesn't matter." He peers beyond me to Derek. "Sorry, man, I'm gonna have to bail early. Bring your truck in tomorrow if you have time, okay?"

"You got it," Derek says, and I shrink as they talk over my head.

Evan glares at me one more time, and then his expression softens a bit. "See ya, Alice. It was nice meeting you."

I can't even look at him. My heart throbs as it pounds, and I have a sudden urge to curl up in a heap and hide under a table. He treated me well, and I treated him like *shit*. And for what? Because I didn't want to explain what a goddamn mess my life is? Because I *really* wanted to go out on a date with him but I'm too scared to get to know him as more than just a pillar of muscle with a nice cock attached?

Because I know he deserves better than what I'll give him, and I just proved that to myself, Derek, *and* the one guy who wanted more from me than a fuck?

Tears blur my vision. I'm hurt, I'm embarrassed, and I'm furious with myself. No wonder I never make it beyond the sex with anyone. I didn't even mean to hurt him. Yet that's exactly what I did. I am a douche.

Evan leaves, and I can barely see through my tears. I hold my breath to keep the cry in, and Derek's hand comes gently to rest on my shoulder.

"Alice?" he says, concern in his tone.

I look away as the tears spill out. God fucking damn it all to hell. "I just need to fix my makeup," I say, forcing chipperness into my tone again. "Hope your buddy isn't pissed at you for this, Derek. I fucked up, and it won't happen again."

I take off toward the winding staircase.

"Alice, wait," Derek calls at my back, but I push through the curtain behind the base of the staircase, hurry down the long hallway of offices, and let myself into my own.

There, I close the door quietly behind myself and sink to the floor. Drawing shaking breaths, I try to pull myself out of the tailspin of emotion.

You're at work, Alice. Suck it up. Suck it up.

It would be so easy to drown the pain with one little swallow and a nice, tall glass of water. I gaze at my makeup stand and the little, locked drawer at the bottom of it. Andee shares my dressing room, but she's never seen inside that drawer.

I push myself to my feet. Thumb the key hanging from my wrist that has my access card to The Core and my identification inside a little plastic sleeve. The little key I've sworn I'd throw away again and again.

Music from the dance floor rushes in as Andee opens the door. "Whew!" She lets out a breath and the scent of vodka follows her into the room. I let go of the key on my wrist and swipe the tears off my cheeks. I'm her friend, her mentor. She can't see me crumbling like this.

"That was a *rough* one!" she says with a laugh. "Get this: They both wanted each other, they both said so, but you know what they were nervous about?"

"What?" I say, taking a few deep breaths to pull my shit together before I let her see my face. I count in my head slowly backward from ten as she talks, willing the tears away.

"Kissing!" Andee cries. "Geoffrey thinks he's a terrible kisser. He didn't want to kiss Brett. So guess what I did?"

The tears are gone, so I plaster my cheer onto my lips and face her, grinning. "What did you do?"

"I kissed them *both* and promised they're both up to snuff. Damn, can gay guys kiss. I have a boner the size of the state and I'm not even a dude."

I burst into laughter. "You're a genius as always, Andee!" I nudge her, and she tilts her head, inspecting me.

"Your makeup. What the hell did you do?"

I was not crying! "Got carried away," I say, dragging a finger across the skin beneath my eye to see how much makeup is really there. I peer into the mirror. "Ew."

"Tall blond, green eyes?" Andee asks, waggling her eyebrows suggestively at me.

My heart clenches at the imagery. "Yeah," I say, managing a giggle. "Evan."

"Did he fuck as good as he looks like he'd fuck?"

"Yeah, it wasn't bad." Wasn't bad? What is wrong with me?! I'm lying to *Andee*.

She grabs a towel from the shelf and turns to the bathroom. "Well, I hope you're all refreshed from it, because I'm taking a shower break. Derek says we have a birthday party coming in."

"Don't worry, Andee," I say. "I've got it. You just chill for a bit."

She flips off her heels and slips into the bathroom. "Wicked. Have fun!"

I finish wiping the makeup off my cheeks and reapply a coat of eyeliner. Three more deep breaths, and I'm ready to hit the dance floor again. No sexy green eyes linger in my thoughts. I glance once more at the locked drawer and then pull myself away. I won't think of that again, tonight. Derek taught me I'm better than my habits. I can't forget it no matter what happens.

The music brings me back to life. I throw myself into the music and lights, spinning, dancing, touching everyone who crashes into me. This is where I belong. I don't want strings holding me down. I can't afford the irrationality that comes with the emotion of it. And as I lose myself in the music, my mood brightens. I'll get the birthday party started, hook up a few people, and then maybe get fucked again myself. This is all I know, and it's what I'm best at.

I spin to the edge of the dance floor and swoop in to greet the ladies just walking through the door. They're in their mid-thirties and one of them is wearing a hideous tiara covered with feathers. The birthday girl!

I greet them all, start scanning the crowd for matches. My eyes fall upon Derek behind the bar, his arms folded across his chest, his eyes hard.

I'll do the best damn job I can. I only hope he's not disappointed in me for what happened. And if he is, I'll do everything I can to fix it, put it behind me, and never think of Evan again.

The dance music pulls us all back into the crowd, and I work my magic matchmaking skills on them all.

Look Who's Here

I roll out of bed and tumble to the floor on my knees. Motherfucker, I must have drunk a lot last night.

The Core's been busier than usual, and Andee and I got talked into a drinking game with a couple of young, rich entrepreneurs on the executive floor. Naturally, we lost, and I don't remember half of the rest of the night. My high heels are still on, and I flip them off, frowning at all the mud caked up the side of one heel. We must have walked home.

Andee and I have shared this apartment for the last three months. It's not big, but it's stylish, and we each have a bedroom with an ensuite bathroom. It's only a few blocks from The Core. I slip into my bathroom and groan at the sight of myself. Makeup is smeared across one of my temples and the back of my hand, and I'm wearing one of Andee's glittery hair pins. When did I put this in?

I strip out of last night's dress and shower, letting the steam soothe away some of the soreness in my shoulders. When I step out of the bathroom, the cool air helps refresh my mood a bit. I slip into the kitchen in my bathrobe. Andee's just crawling out of bed, too. I start the coffee pot and sit at our little kitchen table for two, my throbbing head in my hands, mirroring Andee's position.

A half a pot of coffee—and a few Advil for Andee—later, we're coherent enough for conversation. "Did we walk home?" I ask Andee.

She takes a sip from her steaming mug and shakes back her knotted curls. "Yeah, we stopped at the Quick Shop for scratch tickets. I think I lost mine."

I let out a laugh. "Oh yeah, that's right." I reach for my purse on the counter and dig out the little scratch card. "Huh. I won the chance to play again."

"Aren't you lucky?" she giggles. "Damn. Those rich guys! Dean and... what the hell was his name?"

I ransack my brain but come up blank. "I'll ask Derek. Oh, shit! Derek! We have to apologize. We're not *both* supposed to be shitfaced on the job."

Andee waves the concern off. "Nah, he was laughing at us the whole time. Especially when I got my shoe stuck in a barstool."

She remembers more than I do, but that sounds like it was funny as hell. I snort with laughter and then make my way back to my bedroom.

We're dressed in our best—Andee in a classic little black dress, me in tight jeans and a *very* revealing shirt—when our shift starts at The Core. The lights kill at the same time as the beat hits, and the DJ brings the place to life. My hangover vanishes, and I stride to the door to welcome in the line of patrons waiting outside. I'm gonna do my damn best tonight. Make all my recent bullshit up to Derek. He deserves a better employee than I've been lately.

They start filing in. I'm greeted with smiles, squeals, and affectionate hugs from the men and women who pour through the door. I know most of them, and I've probably made out with at least half. They're what make this place as amazing

31

as it is: the people, the variety, the enthusiasm. They break into dancing the moment they're on the floor, and glasses clink down onto the bar in a familiar rhythm. I glance back at Andee, already hard at work pairing people up, and flash her a smile.

But then I turn back to the door and my good mood evaporates. My heart stalls, and I can't close my mouth.

Shit.

Evan steps into the neon and black-lit glow of The Core, his hands in the pockets of his jeans, his dark, button-down shirt open to the third button. His piercing green eyes meet mine, and a hint of a smile curls up the edges of his lips.

Even as panic grips my throat so I can't speak a word, desire rushes through me like a tsunami. *Evan.* I haven't seen him since that night in the booth... over two weeks ago... and I haven't stopped thinking about him once.

I should turn away. I should walk right the fuck out of this place... lock myself in my changing room until the sun comes up... before he can mess with my head again like he did last time. Or before I can mess with his.

But he just looks so delicious. And the way his eyes glare right into me, loaded with need... he wants me, too. He's here for me.

I should walk away.

Instead, I lick my lips, step forward, and reach out my hand. He takes it—his fingers warm and strong as I remember—and I pull him into The Core.

Ten Minute Break

The way Evan walks toward me is so sexy as his fingers grasp mine, his strides deliberate. His eyes are locked with mine, drilling into me, and my heartbeat kicks up as that sexy, slow smile of his spreads.

"Hey," I say, my voice shaking as he closes the distance between us and snakes his arm around my waist, pulling me close to him. I love being pressed to his chest. He's solid as hell.

"Hey Alice," he says, narrowing his eyes.

I search his gaze. Why is he here again? He didn't like the idea of being paired up with a random stranger last time he was here, so I fucked him in a booth to break the ice. But I liked it so much more than I wanted to admit. Evan's sexy body, the intensity of his green eyes, and the way he makes me feel like I'm the only one here who matters... it was all too much for me to resist. And when I brushed him off like just another one of my many initiation screws, it hurt him. He walked away.

Evan's thumb strokes up and down my back as he holds me so close, my breasts pressed to him. Last time we met, we crushed ourselves together and then crushed each other in every way possible for a one-night fling. Yet he sweeps me into his embrace as if we've both been longing for this, craving it. The intensity of our touch is electric. As he leans closer to me, his lips just a breath away from mine, it's crystal clear: Evan is here for me.

"Did you come back to really give it a try at The Core?" I ask. "Good crowd tonight. I can find you anything you like."

He chuckles, and the sound kicks my nerves into high gear. He's so confident, so cool. "I know you can. But no, I'm good. Came to see you, actually."

I knew it. My breath is shaky. "Evan, I told you before, I can't," I say. There's too much on the line, and my job performance has been shitty enough lately thanks to the way I screwed with both our heads. I've got my heart set on this promotion, and hanging out with Evan isn't going to earn it for me.

"Can't what? Can't stand here in my arms? Seems to be going alright so far." He smirks, and his goddamn grin is so infectious I feel the corner of my lips pull up.

"I'm working," I say.

"I know you are."

"So... you didn't come in with an open mind, tonight?" Even as I say it, the thought clenches in my stomach as a wave of nausea spins through me. I don't want to pair Evan up with someone else here. I don't want to hear the moans of another woman wrapped around his hips. I don't want to see him sweaty and satisfied from someone else.

Evan clicks his tongue. "You know, I thought about it. Thought about asking you to hook me up. I'm into brunettes, not blonds. I wondered if maybe that was my problem last time. But I can't do it, and do you know why?"

"Why?" It's a whisper. I'm terrified of why.

34

"Because I'm not wasting the chance to be with you. I meant what I said: I already see what I want."

Oh my God, his words. He's so thoughtful, so confident. I step back from him, not far enough that he takes his hand off my waist, but far enough that I'm not pressed right up against him anymore. It gives me space to think. "You seem to care a lot about me after just one night," I snap sarcastically.

"With you, Alice, that's all it took."

My skin flushes at his words, and the intensity of his gaze tells me he's not lying. He cares about me. Panic lights and burns inside me as dangerous and hot as my desire. I push Evan's hand off my waist and cross my arms over my chest. "You don't even know me."

"I know." He cocks an eyebrow at me. "I want to get to know you, though."

"We can't do this." I'm so scattered. I want to fight him, to refuse this conversation any longer, but I can't tear my eyes away from him. His gaze is hypnotic. His touch is electric. I want him so badly I *have* to push him away.

"Because you're working. But what about later? We could have a cup of coffee together."

Holy shit, he's asking me out. I gape at him, wordless.

"I don't date."

"So Derek told me. But you know what I decided when I left here that night?"

"What did you decide?" I'm as curious as he is: I want to know Evan, to figure out what makes him tick.

"I decided I don't want to take no for an answer." He steps closer again, looming over me, his breath rustling my hair.

I want so badly to kiss him again. I swallow hard to restrain the urge. "I really don't date, though. Haven't in years. This place is my life."

"But you might, someday," he says, cracking that sexy smile again. "And when you do, if it's not with me, I'll kick my own ass forever for not trying harder when I had the chance."

He talks like I'm some prize. "Why me? Why not one of the many other willing women here who would jump at the chance to take you home?"

Evan slides his hand down my arm, watching my skin prick with goose bumps as he does. When he returns his gaze to mine, it's heated with challenge. "You're an elite, here. Everyone's desire. I don't want to spend my life in regret because I didn't try hard enough to convince you I'm worth your time."

"It isn't you, Evan. Not even a little bit. You're..." I take in the sight of his sculpted chest straining against his shirt, his hard-set jaw, blond hair falling just a little onto his forehead, and piercing green eyes. He's fucking flawless, that's what he is. "I'd date you in a heartbeat, if I could."

"So do it. Date me. Whatever's holding you back can't be so important that you spend your life regretting me, too, can it?"

"Who says I'd regret you?" I try to balk, but it's totally forced.

"Oh, you would," Evan says with an arrogant smirk. There's that confidence again. It takes my breath away.

"Alice," he says, leaning down so his lips graze mine once, softly. He's *so* delicious. "Just go out with me. Just once. We don't even have to repeat our... adventures from the other night." His eyes flash at the memory.

I melt into his kiss. In all my time in The Core, no one has asked me out on a date. Not once. I've had one night stands, five minute flings... and I like it that way. I always know what men and women expect from me: sex. Nothing more. No strings. No complications. And they never want to do me again, either, because I pair them up with someone perfectly compatible to their needs once I've figured them out.

If I go out with Evan, he'll expect we'll do it again. Eventually, he'll tell me about his childhood or something and want me to tell him where I come from, how I ended up as the top matchmaker in The Core.

But while he might think he wants to know those things, he really doesn't. He doesn't want to know how I stumbled, ninety pounds with my skin sagging off me into The Core looking for drugs. How pills weren't enough anymore for a filthy street bum, and I was desperate to find a needle to shove into a vein, a step down a slippery slope I'm so thankful I managed to resist. How Derek fucked me into oblivion and showed me how learning to restrain myself could make me feel more in control—and higher—than anything else.

I've never looked back. Never stopped restraining myself, resisting temptation. I've never taken a pill—Advil aside—or let anyone convince me I'd enjoy letting them into my heart. It's too dark in there to visit again, and I sure as hell don't want to show that part of me to Evan. If I did, he'd be repulsed. I'd rather have him hate me and admire me from afar, than love me and then be disgusted when he gets too close.

But this is a temptation I haven't faced since I locked my pills in a drawer: something I want so badly I can almost taste it. I want Evan. I want to fuck him again, to let him touch me, make me come, and whisper my name when we're spent.

Can I find a way to do this? To let Evan touch me, know me as I am now, without exposing him to all the dark and ugly sides of my seedy past? Can I strike a balance between resistance and submission, getting to know him without letting all that shit spill out?

If I don't try, I'll never escape the remorseful fog of the last two weeks. Every time I've thought his name I've been plunged into regret and shame for hurting someone who only wanted a few more minutes of my time.

I glance around the bar. Derek and Andee are side by side, regarding me with curiosity. Is that disappointment I see on my boss's face? I pull Evan close.

"Meet me at the back of the dance floor by the spiral stairs in an hour. I'll think about it. Okay?"

Evan's face lights with elation. "Sounds great, Alice," he says. God, I love the way he says my name. Like he's tasting me as it rolls across his tongue.

"Alright." My heart flutters with excitement. "See you then." I plant one quick peck on his cheek and then spring into the crowd, dancing, twisting, making new friends and greeting old ones.

Evan wants to date me. I match up two older gentlemen who are looking for more cuddling than anything else, and they slide into a booth together to drink and kiss.

I want to date Evan, too. A young woman is here for her twentieth birthday, and I lead her up the stairs to Christopher as a birthday surprise. He'll take good care of her in one of the elegant, private rooms, and fuck her so hard she'll never forget it.

The hour passes by quickly, and before I know it, I catch Evan's hot gaze peering at me from the shadows beneath the spiral staircase as I descend. My heart skips a beat. I wonder if he's taken his eyes off me the whole night, and decide probably not. His intensity is out of this world. Something so bright, so hot, that I can't resist it. Even if he's a bit demanding, even if he pushes me, I like the way he talks, the way he stares, and that arrogant confidence that just won't relent. Confidence is sexy. And as many times as I try to deny it, it's true: I'm as fascinated with him as he is with me. I hold up a finger to him to ask his patience as I dance across the floor to Andee at the bar.

She's sweaty and carrying a few drinks at once. I take two to help her out... we're not waitresses, but if people are getting cozy and need the alcohol flowing so things move along smoothly, we deliver drinks.

"Where to?" I ask.

"Rooftop," she says. "I've got a fucking orgy going on up there. Three women, four men."

"Nice!" We move toward the elevator. The glass doors slide closed and I flash her a knowing grin as the elevator takes off up the shaft. The first time we were in here together was an orgy, too.

"So, can you do me a favor?" I ask.

Andee blows a strand of her highlighted hair away from her face. "Sure, what's up?"

"I have a girl upstairs with Christopher, but I'm taking a ten minute break. Can you check on her, please?"

Andee raises a suspicious eyebrow at me. "A ten minute break."

"Yes, I'll just be in our changing room." She sees right through me, dammit.

"Sure. Just promise me you'll fill me in on all the delicious Evan details when you're done."

I roll my eyes. "It's just another fuck. He's infatuated with me, so I'm trying to cool him off in the nicest way possible, you know?"

Andee laughs. "Oh, Alice."

"What?" I laugh with her.

She faces me, her expression one of delight mixed with something I can't quite pinpoint. Concern? Sympathy?

"Just let it happen," she says. "You like him. I know you well enough—and I know *people* well enough, after all my time here—to tell that from across the club. You don't need to hide it from me."

I feel my face flush, and I nod, looking away. "I'm sorry. I just don't really know what to do about all this. I didn't want you to think I'm not taking work seriously, you know? He's stubborn, though."

"And so are you. Take your ten minute break, I'll keep an eye on things. Take twenty if you want to." She winks at me, and for the millionth time since I found Andee slinging coffee out a drive-through window wearing blue mascara, I'm so grateful for her friendship. She's one of a kind, and I'm lucky to have her.

More Than Ten Minutes

Evan is right where I left him when the elevator touches down. The orgy upstairs is in full swing, and Derek's behind the bar, socializing. The dance floor is alive, moving to its own rhythm. I approach Evan with caution, nervous. How fast can my heart thrum, really? I try to will myself to calm down.

"Hey," he greets me the same way he always does.

"Hey yourself," I say. "Um, want to come with me for a minute? Just to somewhere quieter."

He grins, and something about his posture changes. It's that confidence surging forth, and it zaps my thoughts into oblivion. I want to touch him. To taste his intensity. I take his hand and lead him through the black curtain into the office hallway, unlocking my dressing room door. Inside, I can smell the candle Andee burned in here earlier: apple cinnamon, sweet and tangy in the air. Evan slips in behind me and closes the door.

"So," he says, "are you gonna take me up on that date?"

I bite my lip, shake my head. His expression falls.

I can hear the disappointment in his tone. "What did you want to talk about, then?"

I wring my fingers together as I turn to fully face him. He takes in my figure in tight jeans and his breath hitches. I meet his eyes. My voice is rough with desire. "I don't want to talk at all."

He squints for a moment, perplexed, and then recognition lights his face and he rushes at me. Swoops me into his arms, lifts me into the air, and I wrap my legs around his waist.

"Alice," he groans, kissing me. His lips are sweet, fresh mint on his breath, and his hands slide over my backside. He pulls me against him, his fingers possessive, and I twist my fingers in his hair. I lap at his tongue with mine, earning a groan that rumbles through his solid chest.

Evan spins me toward the couch and crushes me down against it, his body between my legs. He hardens as I moan into his kiss, and I writhe up against him, eager to feel all of him. I reach for the edge of his shirt and he stops me with a firm hand on my wrist.

I hesitate, pulling away to take in his expression. It's hard, unreadable. Why?

"Sorry," he murmurs. "Not here."

I blink with surprise. He looks worried. Where's that confidence I adore? "Okay," I say. I stroke my hand down his cheek to soothe his stress. We can stay dressed. Easier to throw clothes back on quickly if we have to, if someone walks in.

His worried look is replaced by a wash of hunger as he dives for my mouth again. I take his kiss eagerly, running my fingertips over his abs through his shirt. My God, he's solid. I love the way his muscles heave against me as he breathes, a groan in every draw of breath. He reaches up and smoothes a strand of my hair away from my face, and then trails his fingertips down to my neck. He pulls aside the strap of my tank top and kisses me all along my neck, my shoulder. His mouth is so hot it fires desire, hot and liquid, through my body. I press my hips up against him, and he presses back.

"Evan," I groan, dragging my fingernails through his hair again. "Take me."

"Slowly, Alice," he says. "Slowly this time."

Oh, God, yes.

He slips his hand beneath my shirt and strokes my skin with his thumb, still pressing against me, rock hard through his jeans and mine. He moves up to my breast and slides his fingers beneath my bra, taking my nipple between his first two fingers. The touch sends an electric jolt down between my legs, and I arch up, calling out. He loses his breath and does it again, and again, and I'm lost in ecstasy, panting. I kiss him desperately, needing more of his touch, more of his mouth.

He gives it to me, kissing down my neck once more and then yanking my shirt harshly aside to expose my breast. The cool air perks my nipple and he takes it in his mouth, sucking, groaning, his eyes knit shut. He loves this. I can feel it in the way he rocks against me. A shudder of the most delicious agony—the need for more—rolls through my body, and it only encourages him. He sucks my nipple again.

Evan kisses down to my stomach and places a tender kiss on my bellybutton, and I laugh, squirming at the tickle. He grins deviously. "I love that," he says, his voice husky with arousal. "Your giggle." He kisses me again, and I'm helpless to the giggles that shake my body.

He moves lower, snaps open the button on my jeans, and tugs down the zipper. My laughter ceases as I realize he's really going down there. I'm going to fuck him again. I lift my hips as he shifts his weight off me so he can slide the rough denim over my ass, and I kick the jeans away. He steadies my hips with his hands for a moment, and then pulls my panties to the side, revealing me.

His breath rushes over me and I cry out, suddenly nervous, but all my nerves vanish when his mouth connects with my skin. He kisses once, and then wraps his lips around my clit and licks it very slowly up and down. His mouth is hot as it strokes that perfect spot that I jump with every lick, my hands knotted in his hair. He parts his lips further, sliding his tongue down and back up, and pleasure rushes over me so intense I can't loosen my fingers from his hair. He licks again, and I moan. Again. Again. I'm lost in this intensity, electricity crackling through me every time the hot texture of his tongue slides over the sensitive bud.

"Evan," I whimper.

He doesn't answer. Just keeps licking. I close my eyes, the sensation pushing me closer to the edge, and he groans against me, his breath so hot on my thighs I think I'm going to combust. He licks faster, my wetness coating both of us. It's the sexiest thing, watching him do this just for me, feeling nothing but pleasure because *he* wants to give it to me. Lightning rips through me as my legs tense, my toes curling. He reaches up and finds my nipples with his fingertips, pinching them, licking faster. I hold my breath as the pressure builds, my hips lifting to offer more of me to his mouth, and he receives it, sweeping his tongue up my slit from the bottom to the top once, twice...

And then I come hard, shrieking as I tug on his hair, my hips bucking against his mouth. Evan groans and cups my ass, pulling me up to his mouth as he licks me through every throb of my orgasm. I gasp, try to come down from the peak, but he just keeps licking.

Again and again he licks, holding me up in the air as the strength in my legs gives out, my body surrendering to the pleasure. Evan begins circles over my clit with his tongue, around and around, his eyes closed as he tastes me. Heat swells within me again and I hold my breath, reaching up to clench the cushion above my head, and then I crash once more, a second orgasm pulsing through me. I'm helpless in his hands, lost in orgasm, spasms rocking my body so hard my head swims.

Evan lowers my hips and releases me, licking his lips once. They look swollen, and I reach out to kiss him, so he swipes his hand over his mouth and chin to clean my wetness off and then dives forward to take my lips. I whimper into his mouth, letting him run his tongue over my lower lip just as he did to my sex.

"Condom," he growls.

I can't find words. I just point, kind of frantically waving my finger at my dressing table. He pushes away from me and turns, and I hear something rattle. I open my eyes and he's jiggling the bottom drawer, trying to open it.

"Not that one!" I shout, sitting upright. Panic scatters my thoughts as Evan gazes at me in shock at the severity of my reaction.

"Not that one," I repeat, trying to catch my breath. My pulse thuds in my ears as I feel my skin flush hot. Shit. "Sorry. Top drawer."

Evan hesitates for a moment, regarding me warily, but then slides open the top drawer and pulls out a condom. Relief washes away my fear and I smile as he returns to the couch, unzipping his jeans.

He's so long. Not too thick, but just the right shape: thicker at the head than the base. I reach out and take him in my hand, gripping him, and he loses his breath as he fumbles with the condom.

I take it from his fingers and rip it open with my teeth. I roll it on for him, admiring him again, and then Evan can't wait anymore. He pushes me back on the couch, spreads my legs wide with his hands, grabs hold on my thighs, and drives himself into me.

I call out. Lift my hips off the cushions and receive every inch of him. He slides in deep and hard, impacting the back of me. I'm already sensitive from orgasm and soaking wet. He closes his eyes, still braced high above me, and I get a good look at the shape of his body. Damn, I wish he had his shirt off.

He pulls back to the head of his cock and then slides back into me. It sends a rush of arousal through my body, tingling all the way down to my toes, and I let my breath out in a moan. Evan leans down to kiss me again, his mouth worshipful on mine, as he withdraws and thrusts in once more.

He doesn't speed up. Just slowly pulls out, kissing me the whole time, and then pushes in. Over and over he repeats this torturous, tantalizing motion, sliding along just the right spot, his hands trailing over my breasts, my hips. "Alice," he whispers between kisses. "Oh, baby, you feel so good."

I'm unraveled by his words. I raise my hips to meet his, and he falls into a rhythm of these slow, deliberate thrusts. Each time he pushes into me is as fulfilling as the first time, like I've missed him inside my body and finally have him back. I whimper, closing my eyes, the intensity overwhelming me. He feels so good. So fucking good.

Evan slips both his hands on either side of my face and holds me there as he kisses me. He pulls back to look at me as he gives another thrust, and I cry out. I can't stare into his eyes. It's too intense. But he watches me as he fucks me, his hands on my cheeks, kissing me with every thrust.

And then it builds in me once more, the orgasm pushing closer as he thrusts, and when he pulls out to the head and hesitates, I'm brimming over with agony and pleasure. He holds there for a moment, watching me, and then drives it in hard and fast. I gasp, and he jams himself into me in a fast and relentless rhythm, pounding, his hardness pushing me over the edge. I clench around him, my mind fogging over with ecstasy as he finally hits that speed I've craved. My sensitivity triples and before I can think a third orgasm crushes me from the inside out, and Evan growls sharply.

"Yes," he says, panting as he fucks me hard. "Yes."

46

I quiver around him, and I feel him thicken as his own orgasm impends. I reach up and thread my fingers into his hair again, lifting my head to reach his lips. He takes my kiss and groans into my mouth, his length moving in and out of me, and then he gives one final, hard thrust and loses himself between my legs. I kiss him mercilessly, needing all of his mouth I can get, needing every drop of his pleasure he's willing to give me.

And then he rests against me, and we're still kissing. We don't stop even as our heartbeats slow. It just feels right, his lips moving along mine, my mouth receiving his tongue. He kisses me like he's never enjoyed something so much before, his eyes knit closed, never breaking to come up for air.

I come down from the high slowly, my body weak beneath his. He's hot on top of me, heavy and secure. I love this feeling. I run my hands through his hair. Slowly, concern bleeds into my mood. We're still kissing.

This wasn't a hookup. This wasn't a one-night-stand or a five minute fuck.

This was more than sex.

This was something so much more I can't quite wrap my head around it. Alarm registers in my head and I break the kiss, staring into Evan's eyes with shock.

What did we just do?

I Can't Resist

Evan frowns as I search his eyes. "What's wrong, baby?" He's still out of breath, his voice a low, satisfied growl.

I stare into those green eyes. The first time we had sex, I came twice and missed him when he was gone. Here in my dressing room, I came three times and can't bear to stop tasting him. What is happening between us? This isn't how it's supposed to go.

But it feels so good. I kiss him again, and he's the one who pulls away from me, confusion clear across his face.

"Alice, tell me what's wrong."

I don't know how to explain to him that everything we've done is wrong, and yet feels so right I can't deny it. I want more of Evan. I want this again and again with him. I want his touch, his kiss, his words, his intensity. I need to know him. What is it that makes him touch me as though he's afraid it's the last time? Why does he make love to me like he's making the most of every moment in case it never happens again?

Is that what we did? Did we make love, instead of just fucking?

Maybe when I cast him out last time, it wounded him so deeply he thinks I'll do it again. And as he brushes a sweaty strand of hair away from my forehead, concern etched across his gorgeous features, I realize that's probably exactly it. He's terrified of the words I'll say next. He's probably bracing himself for my cold dismissal, as I did last time.

But I can't dismiss the first man I've had *more than sex* with. Derek and I connected, but on a mentor-friend level, not like this. This is something else... something precious, something I don't want to let go.

"Baby," Evan urges, and that fear is plain in his eyes. "What did I do? Talk to me."

I shake my head. Run my fingers through his hair again--God, it's so soft—and take a deep breath. "I think I'd like you to take me on a date, if you still want to," I say. My voice shakes. I want this as desperately as he does.

Joy breaks across Evan's face like sunrise, his grin boyish and excited. "Alright," he says. "I'll plan it out. When do you have time off?"

I kiss him again, tasting his happiness through the smile on his lips. "I'm off Monday and Tuesday nights. Sunday I do inventory, so..."

"Monday it is," Evan finishes. "Great. I'll pick you up here, if that's cool."

My heart is sprinting with delight. I'm really going to go on a date with Evan. He withdraws from me and tucks himself away, and I toss the condom in the garbage and try to reassemble my clothing. It's no use: he fucked me with my panties on, so I need a shower and a change of clothes. I clench deep down inside, a delicious tenderness there reminding me of what we just did, and how incredibly well he did it.

I walk Evan to the door without my jeans on. He wraps his arms around me and breathes deeply at my hair. I crane up to kiss him again, and when our lips part, it aches a little bit. I want all night with him, but I have to get back to work.

"See you Monday night," Evan says, squeezing my hand.

"Bye," I say.

Evan slips out the door, and I'm about to close it when his hand shoots through the crack between the door and the frame, stopping me. I jump with surprise and he pushes back into the room, taking my face between his hands. He kisses me deep, his tongue sweeping into my mouth, and I drop my jeans from my fingertips and just take in every sensation. His breath, his tongue, his body against mine. It's official: Evan is perfect.

He breaks the kiss with a look of sorrow on his face. "Okay. For real this time. See you Monday night." His cocky smirk is back, and I can't help but giggle.

"Okay, go," I say. This time, he does.

I close the door and take a moment to collect my thoughts. I strip off my clothes and toss them in a heap, and my eyes fall upon my bottom drawer. Thank God he didn't open it. Evan doesn't need to know those things. He's too amazing, and he thinks I'm amazing, so I'm not about to kill his impression of me. Nope, I'm Alice the matchmaker, not Alice the junkie or Alice the thief. That bullshit is far enough in the past I can bury it all and just let him enjoy me for who I am now.

I'm just shaking a bobby pin out of my hair when the door clicks open. I let out a quiet laugh. "How did you get in?" I say, expecting to see Evan when I turn.

But of course it isn't Evan. It's Andee, her jaw dropped, and I'm naked as the day I was born sporting nothing but a freshly-fucked hairstyle.

"I have a keycard, you love-struck sex fiend," Andee says, excitement radiating into the room. "And you need to give me *all* the details."

I burst into laughter as she closes the door behind herself. I'll give her details later. Evan fucked the hell out of me in all the best ways I can imagine, and Andee will be ecstatic to hear it all.

And I'm going to go out with Evan. I can't wait to see him again, to taste all he has to offer, and to show him all the sides of me he'll adore. Maybe we'll go back to his place. Maybe he'll make me come four times like he boasted he could do. Maybe I'll fall asleep in his arms and feel the rise and fall of his delicious chest until the sun comes up.

For now, I'm going to hop into the shower to imagine Evan's hands all over me as the heat cascades down.

Ride Of My Life

I lean against the concrete wall outside The Core. This place is home in so many ways, but I'm rarely *outside* it. I bend and pick up a discarded paper bag from the sidewalk and toss it in the garbage can. I don't appreciate trash laying around, muddying up the atmosphere.

After all, I once *was* that trash, and Derek scooped me up and helped shape me into something new. The person I am now. I swallow hard, try to discard the memory of sitting here homeless and cold, begging for change to get my next fix.

The engine of a truck roars around the corner, and my heart sprints with excitement. I have no idea what Evan drives. But the black truck that rolls up and stops is Derek's, and he steps out wearing his jeans and a jersey, looking dark and delicious as always.

"Alice," he says as he locks his doors. "What are you doing here?"

Shit, I don't have a lie ready for this. And I don't really want to lie to Derek anyways... but what will he think if I tell him the truth? He hasn't judged me, I remind myself, not once in all he's seen of my highs and lows. I let out a nervous laugh. "Oh, you know. Nothing much. How about you?" It's Monday. We're never here on Mondays.

Derek sighs. "Taxes. If you shoved me into traffic right now, it wouldn't hurt my feelings one bit."

I glance down the street. "Sorry, boss. Can't help you. If I see a bus coming, I'll be sure to trip you off the curb."

"Perfect." He laughs. "So what do you need? It's your day off."

I bite my lip. "Um, I don't need anything, actually. I'm meeting someone."

His chocolate eyes light with surprise. "Really? Like, a date?"

I nod, my face flushing hot. "Yeah. Um, it's with Evan?" It comes out like a question, like I'm seeking his approval. I suppose I am, in a way. I respect Derek, and Evan is his friend. This is so abnormal for me.

Derek presses his lips together in a line. "I see. He'll be here soon?"

I glance at my phone. "Yep, any minute now."

His expression is stern and unreadable. Is he disappointed in me for dating his friend? Worried I'll reveal to Evan what a fuck up I am, and completely tarnish the reputation of Derek's company? *Not a chance in hell of that happening.* Angry that I'm dating someone I met here? My mind churns over the possibilities, and I clench my phone so hard I'm afraid the battery will pop out.

"Well, have fun," Derek says, moving for the door handle.

That's it? I gulp. "Thanks," I say, my voice a tiny squeak.

Derek pushes through the door. "Oh, Alice," he calls back, catching the door before it swings all the way closed behind him.

"Yes, Derek?"

He sighs again, studying me long and hard before he speaks. "I mean it. Have fun."

Relief pulses through me. "Thanks," I repeat.

"And we should have a meeting on Wednesday before your shift to discuss a few things. Come in an hour early." He vanishes into the building, and my relief shatters. Oh, fucking fuck. He's not pleased. I'm going to get fired.

A snarl down the street catches my attention, distracting me from the anxiety clutching my heart. What the hell is that? A motorcycle rips up behind the giant, black truck, and my jaw falls open as the man steps off—dressed in nicely fitting, faded blue jeans and a black leather jacket—and removes his helmet.

It's Evan. On a fucking motorcycle. My pulse kicks up with fear at the same time as arousal washes through me down low. Of course he rides a motorcycle. He hangs his helmet, grins, and walks slowly toward me, sliding his hand along the box of Derek's truck with approval as he does. Everything about him screams *I am going to fuck you until you claw my back open.*

"Ready to go?" Evan asks, his hair falling just a tiny bit onto his forehead. His green eyes are expectant, excited, and I step closer, inhaling the smell of his leather jacket. No wonder he smelled so good before... when he was locked between my legs... God. The things this man does to me inside.

"I didn't know you had a bike," I say.

"There's lots you don't know about me," Evan says. "I can show you a few things, if you like."

I glance at the motorcycle. I've never been on one before.

Evan extends his hand to take mine. "Come on. I don't want to waste a second with you."

His words. His unbelievably romantic words. His natural cool, his sexy exterior... I suddenly don't want to waste a second with Evan, either. I slide my hand into his, and he clasps me tightly. I don't ever want to let him go.

He slips a helmet over my head and positions me behind him on the motorcycle. I wrap my arms around his waist and lean against his back, and he takes a moment to rub the back of my hand as I hold him. "You good?"

"I'm more than good," I say, stroking his abs with my thumbs, and he fires up the engine, pulling out onto the street so fast my stomach lurches.

He doesn't have to warn me: I know it's true. I'm in for the ride of my life tonight.

On The Edge

The roar of the motorcycle is exhilarating. I can't stop grinning, and though I trust Evan knows what he's doing, my pulse kicks into high gear as we round a corner on a green light. We lean so far on the curve.

"Don't mind a scenic ride, do you?" Evan calls over his shoulder.

I shake my head and shout back. "Not at all!" The longer I get to spend straddling Evan's hog, the better. I giggle quietly at my own internal innuendo. I'm such a dork. At least I didn't say it out loud.

We cruise through the rest of the stoplights, and Evan points out the auto shop he works at, called Meyer's. We hit the highway, and I hang on tighter as Evan guns the engine up over the speed limit. There's no traffic this direction on a Monday afternoon, so he breezes along beside rare other cars with ease. Eventually, he slows and pulls into a turnout lane, and takes us out onto a scenic highway that winds along the base of the mountains and even ascends up into them, if we stay on it long enough. Where in the world is he taking me? A million date clichés run through my mind: a picnic, a boat ride on a lake.

Maybe my expectations are too high thanks to my sad lack of dating experience and the lame setups in movies. Maybe the bike ride *is* the date. I'm actually kind of relieved by the idea. This is so nice, so low-pressure, just holding onto Evan as he rides. He's relaxed in his posture, occasionally letting one hand off the bike to clasp mine around his middle. I like the feel of him breathing in my arms. The memory of his body over mine as he breathes harshly, lost in orgasm, surges into my thoughts. If tonight goes well, maybe we'll do that again. But for now, I'm happy wrapped around him like this, the noise of the engine drowning out the sounds of the world around us.

This is what Evan loves. This is where he's most comfortable, the passion that drives him. He winds us up the highway, daringly close to a barricaded edge that drops down so sharply my stomach falls into my feet as I stare. We're climbing into the mountains as we ride. The drop-off disappears from my view—thankfully—when we enter more tree-covered area. But my excitement doesn't dwindle as I take in the scenery. It's beautiful out here, exhilarating in the rushing breeze as Evan speeds up yet again. And my arms are around a man whose intensity is luring me in moment by moment. I'm so delighted, so free, that I laugh aloud, sliding my hand up to the middle of Evan's chest. I feel him hum with pleasure as I press my palm to his heart, and I snuggle closer to his back.

He points off to the side into a clearing. The leaves are in full springtime bloom, the meadows dotted with emerging yellow flowers, and in the midst of the clearing two deer munch on the lush grass. I watch them until they vanish behind tree cover again, and then Evan tilts his head back to talk to me once more.

"I come out here every weekend in the summer," he explains. "I love the ride, and I love the wildlife. I go a little faster when I don't have a girl on the back of the bike that I'm trying not to frighten away."

"You're not frightening me," I say. I adore his daring edge.

I can hear the wicked grin in his words. "Really? Okay."

Oh, shit! Evan pushes the engine faster, and I squeal with a mixture of delight and utter terror. Evan laughs, panic flipping in my chest as we round over a short hill. We're upon it and gone so fast my head spins, and the next incline is even sharper. We wind up the mountain to a dizzying, daunting height, the other mountains beside this one shrinking away as we climb. It's breathtaking, but I can't look at the sharp drops full of boulders that have crumbled off the mountainside over time, and I don't dare to peer up to see where they fell from. I press my helmeted cheek to Evan's back and close my eyes, trying to shove my stomach back down where it belongs. *I will not barf. I will not barf.*

We slow, and I open my eyes. Evan turns the bike, gently pulling into a parking lot. I look around, surprised to see a dangling sign that says "The Hideaway." It looks like a little, old-west-themed bed and breakfast nestled into the quiet side of one of the mountains. We stop in a parking space and Evan kills the engine. The sudden silence almost dizzies me more, so I don't let go of him just yet.

Evan pulls his helmet off. "We're here, baby," he says. "Didn't go too fast, did I?"

I'm not this fragile, I tell myself as I'm still looking for pieces of my stomach somewhere down in my toes. "Not at all," I say, hopping off the motorcycle. My balance is nowhere to be found, though—maybe it's back there munching buttercups in the deer meadow—and I stumble forward.

"Whoa," Evan says as he catches me. I clutch his shoulders, panting, and he helps me get the helmet off. "Easy, baby. You're on solid ground now."

Goddammit. This is pathetic.

He chuckles as he pulls my forehead to rest against his shoulder. The leather cools my hot skin, soothing away some of the nausea but none of the embarrassment.

"So you're an adrenaline junkie?" I say after a few slow breaths, trying to make him think about anything other than how *lame* I am right now.

"Yeah, I guess. The thrill-seeking type. Drives my dad crazy."

"I bet it does." My own thrill-seeking behavior sent my mother running screaming away from me. But then, motorcycles and drugs are two very different thrills. I shake the thought off and lift my head, my balance creeping up apologetically behind me. "Do you skydive and swim with sharks, too?"

He gives me a sheepish shrug. "I've done both. And hang-gliding. Oh, you'd *love* hang-gliding. Can I take you, sometime?"

I let out a nervous laugh and finally manage to meet his green eyes, which shimmer with joy in the late afternoon sun. "Let's work up to that gradually, okay?"

"That wasn't a no, so I'll take it!" Evan says, breaking into a grin so brilliant I want nothing more than to kiss him.

So I do. I kiss him gently at first, just tasting his lower lip, and when I pull away his eyes burn with that intensity, that need. He scoots back on the seat, tugs me forward, so I climb between Evan and the handlebars to straddle him, and then he crushes my mouth with his. His tongue invades my lips as his hand moves up to cradle the back of my head, holding me there. I can't move away. Not that I want to... not at all. I sigh into his kiss and he pulls on my lower back with his other hand, grinding against me, kissing me harder.

When we finally come up for air, my lips are tender from the roughness of his kiss. Here, in his comfort zone, chasing mountains on his bike, all of Evan's caution is gone.

His eyes penetrate into me as I pant, and he seizes my mouth again, taking my head with both hands. I'm lost in his kiss, the roughness of need in it. I can hardly breathe between the possessive motions of his mouth. He captures my lips and refuses to release them, sliding the tip of his tongue over soft skin. The sun beats hotly on us, and Evan's breath quickens.

He finally pulls away, still holding my head in his hands. God, I love the way he grabs me like this. I'm his prisoner, and there's nowhere I'd rather be. I look away from the intensity of his gaze, peering down at my legs straddling his.

He touches my chin with a fingertip and pulls me up, forcing me to drink in those greens. He's too perfect, especially wearing that aroused flush in his cheeks from our kiss. "Why do you do that?" he asks.

"Do what?" I grimace, a wave of self-consciousness interrupting my blissful admiration of him. I'm so out of my element, romanced by the scenery and probably kissing like a love-struck teenager with no skill whatsoever.

Evan leans closer, lets his lips just brush over mine, and then meets my eyes again. "You don't let me look at you, Alice."

I swallow hard and glance at The Hideaway's swinging sign. Evan tugs on my chin with his fingertips.

"See? Like that. You pull away."

"I don't know," I manage, my voice thick. I really don't. He's just a lot to take in at once.

"Look at me," he insists.

I do, and then I giggle nervously and look away again, but he just waits patiently for me to return my gaze to his. When I do, he searches my eyes, and a rush of fear overcomes me. Can he see that I'm just a fucked up junkie hiding behind all my careful composure? Can he see me through the makeup, the clothes, through all I do at The Core?

It dawns on me that maybe more than my private shame, I'm embarrassed to be leading Evan on. We're already talking about a second date. Hang-gliding, for fuck's sake. Evan can't date me. Part of my job is my openness. How can any man want to be with me, knowing I might be flirting with another man the next night, or grinding on the dance floor with two? Hell, I can't even promise I won't be involved with an orgy later this week. I lick my lips. I have to say this. He can see it's brewing inside of me, I know it. I have to get this off my shoulders.

But Evan sighs before I speak and shakes his head. "My God, Alice, do you have any idea how beautiful you are? No, beautiful doesn't cover it. How perfect you are for me?"

I feel like I've been dropped off one of those cliffs back there. I'm winded by him once again, in all the best and worst ways at once. "How can you say that? You don't know me that well."

"I don't need to. Each moment I spend with you proves what I've thought all along: everything you are is perfect for me, Alice. I have no idea what you like to do, what you like to eat, where you grew up, or what your political views are. None of it will change how I feel about you, because it's all *you*. I can't wait to discover everything I can about you.. Every exciting part that you'll let me see."

He dives forward and kisses me again, and this time, I'm the one who grabs him and holds him there. I cling to Evan like he's a safety net and kiss him like he's unconditional, like no matter what I tell him he'll still want me the way he does now. I know it's false. I know I'm fooling myself. Nothing is unconditional. But for right now, here in the mountains where even the sounds of our lips connecting echo in the vast space between peaks, I want to believe it. Evan. Flawless, intense, thrill-seeking Evan. He's one of a kind, and I'm the one who's going to break his heart someday.

A strange excitement flutters in my chest. Derek wants to meet with me. The Core is my world, my life, and I don't want to leave it behind, but if he fires me, I will have to seek a different job. One that doesn't involve all the male attention, one that wouldn't make me *cheat* on Evan. My excitement mixes with fear: I haven't been apart from The Core or the security of Derek's teaching since my sober life began. Can I hack it in the real world without them? Do I want to?

Will Andee be disappointed in me?

I pour all my worry into Evan's kiss, and he growls as he wraps his arms around me, his hands splayed out across my sides. He grabs me like he'd be willing to strip my clothing off in the parking lot and fuck me on the gravely pavement if it were dark out.

He sighs against me, and then rests his forehead against mine.

"What was that for?" Evan asks.

I shake my head. "I don't know how to let you see me. But maybe I can let you *feel* me, for now. You do things to me, Evan. You make me come alive in all these frightening ways. You make me almost believe I'm as amazing as you say I am."

"You doubt that?" he asks, pulling back to search my eyes. "Alice, everyone in The Core has eyes for you. Why would you doubt that?"

I take a deep breath, try to shed the melancholy hanging over my thoughts as I consider how drastically Evan's presence has changed my view already. I manage a chuckle and climb off his motorcycle. "Is this a restaurant and a hotel?"

Evan almost does a double-take as I change the subject so quickly, but he doesn't sound offended. "Yep, The Hideaway. Amazing food. The chef here had a New York restaurant but hated the noise, so he lets a TV crew film a cooking show here. That keeps the income flowing in."

"Wow. Do you know the chef?"

"I've given him my thanks a time or two for a good meal. I eat here every weekend."

He climbs off his bike, pockets his keys, and then takes my hand. He kisses my knuckles once, piercing me with that green gaze I adore before he leads us across the parking lot.

Push Me

Evan scoots my chair out for me inside the restaurant. Of course he does, I think as I slide into the chair. The décor in here is so homey and country, all lace tablecloths and old-timey accents on the walls. An antique butter churn perches on a ledge near the bar beside a mounted washing board. It's so different than The Core. I wonder how long it's been since I left the city and took in the sights of some place new, and can't remember. I don't think I've done anything like this since before it all fell apart. Before The Core, before the drugs that crushed my spirit and left me empty on Derek's doorstep looking for my next fix.

"You like it here?" Evan asks as he leans his elbows on the table, the glow of the candle centerpiece warming his expression.

I'm still smiling. "It's beautiful," I say, admiring the carved, cherry-wood staircase that winds up to the second floor at the end of the restaurant. It's elegant, and I wonder if it leads to the hotel rooms above. "It reminds me of my grandmother's house when I was growing up. She kicked the bucket years ago though."

Evan frowns as I say it, and I grimace, but the waiter arrives with menus before I have a chance to apologize for being so crass. Evan orders water, and I order a glass of white wine. I haven't had wine in a long time, but I like the light, crisp taste once in a while. It's usually vodka with Andee, so I drink what she drinks.

"Are you not drinking?" I ask.

Evan shakes his head and opens his menu. "Nope. Gotta drive a girl home later, and I kind of like her a lot, so I'm not risking her life."

I glance at the staircase again. We're not getting a room, then. I can't deny I've got a little pang of disappointment, but this is a first date after all. I shouldn't expect so much. Even though we've already fucked twice, dammit. What would be the harm in getting a room? We might have more earth-shattering, knee-buckling sex. *Oh, darn, wouldn't want that to happen.*

"What's good here?" I ask Evan.

He closes his menu and leans forward, silent until I look at him. "Now you're irritated. Why? Would you like to stay the night?"

Apparently I didn't hide my disappointment as well as I thought I did. "I thought you would want to."

"I do. But you were reluctant to go out with me in the first place, so I don't want to push you away by moving too fast."

"We don't have to stay," I rush. "It really is fine. The rooms are probably expensive. And I'm sorry I wasn't eager to go out with you. I wanted to, I just sort of suck at conversation, which you've probably noticed." I'm fumbling through everything, and I'm starting to fear Evan will write me off as way-too-high-maintenance if I keep running my mouth. "What's good here?"

Evan frowns at me, and then he looks back at his menu. "Everything. Whatever you like, they'll make it well."

"I think I'll have the crabcakes," I say. "I'm a sucker for shellfish."

Evan laughs, and I cringe again. The shit that flies out of my mouth. God.

The waiter returns, and I order my crabcakes. He asks for Evan's order, and he regards me for a moment. Then, he shakes a finger at me and gives me the most dead-serious glare he's given me yet.

"No laughing," he says.

I tilt my head, perplexed, as he turns back to the waiter.

"I'll have the sizzling fish tacos," Evan says.

Now I'm the one biting my tongue hard. Dirty retorts fly through my head at lightning speed, and I take a sip of my wine to keep my mouth busy so I can't let any of them slip beyond my lips.

Evan's not done yet. "Can you make a request of the chef for me?" he says. "I'd like extra jalapenos... at least twenty of them, and a side of hot chili sauce, and that lime wasabi sauce of yours, too." He winks at me, and murmurs, "Their wasabi sauce is the best."

Holy shit! The man likes his spice. The waiter cocks an eyebrow and makes a comment about Evan being a daring one. Hell yeah, he is. Thrill-seeking, spicy-hot Evan, the man who has eyes only for me.

The waiter takes our menus, but Evan stops him before he leaves. "One more thing... do you have open rooms in the hotel tonight?"

The waiter nods. "Yes, sir, plenty. Monday nights are quiet around here."

"Great," Evan says, flashing him an elated smile. "Then I'll have a whiskey on the rocks too, please."

My heart flips over once with excitement. We're staying the night. I sip my wine again, grinning from ear to ear, and Evan sits back to gauge my reaction. I'm more than pleased. I'm ecstatic. God, the way he looks at me is infectious. He radiates desire, and it makes me want nothing more than his body naked and tangled with mine, over and over again.

"How long have you worked at Meyer's?" I ask, trying to wrestle my urges under control. Staring at Evan is like dangling meat in front of a tiger: I want him so badly, and every sip of wine I take prods and pokes at the hungry cat within me.

"Since I was fifteen," he explains. "Actually, I bought the place from my dad last year."

I almost choke on my drink. "You own it?"

He nods, grinning at my surprise. "Evan Meyer," he says. "My dad let me work there while I was going through school, and when I got my degree we worked out a deal. He still manages the books for me. He misses my mom too much since she died, and he won't ever sell the house or anything like that, so he, you know, kind of lives off my income. But we're close, it's cool."

Wow. It *is* cool. I had no idea he owned the shop. Derek never said anything about it. "That's really amazing, Evan. He's lucky to have you. I'm sorry about your mom."

"Thanks," he says. "Cancer got her five years ago."

I don't know what to say. Loss like that is something I haven't experienced.

"What about you? Did you go to college?"

That old regret in my heart wakes up and turns my brewing arousal into embarrassment. "No. Um, other things got in the way. I wanted to, though. I still hope maybe I will someday. I'd like to get a degree in business management, but that's as far as my plans ever went."

"What got in the way?" He leans forward, hanging onto my every word.

He's so open, so interested. It would be easy to tell him all of it. How that first pill at age sixteen felt so good I took a second, how I figured spending a week hopped up on painkillers that weren't prescribed to me was okay, as long as it didn't go on longer than that. How I didn't realize I was a hopeless addict even when my mother threw a duffel bag of clothes on the lawn and moved away when I still didn't clean myself up. How I only recognized how far I'd fallen as I slipped a pill into my mouth in my dealer's filthy bathroom with another junkie passed out beside the toilet, and had to step over her vomit pile to get to the sink and swallow the thing with a handful of rusty water.

But if I started to open this can of worms, I'd have to let it all out, and I can't bring myself to tell him how I paid for that pill. Hell, I won't even share that with Andee. This isn't an exciting story worth his attention and intensity. This is a stupid tale of how I wrecked my own life.

"Just life, you know," I lie. "I went to The Core, I got a job, and... I guess time has just slipped by."

"You're what, twenty-two?"

"Yeah," I say. "And you?"

"Twenty-six," Evan says. "You can still go to college, Alice. You'd love it."

"I know. Andee—the other matchmaker, my friend—she's in school. She wants to be a dentist, but I think she might change her mind."

"That's the beauty of college. You can change your mind if you want to."

I nod, but I don't feel the hope of his words in my heart. Now I have bills to pay, expectations and standards to hold myself up to. And college kids party so much. I don't know that I could stay diligent and sober in that kind of environment.

"Tell me about your parents. Do they live near you?"

I swallow the last of my wine and shake my head. A disdainful laugh escapes my mouth. "No, no they don't. Um, we don't speak."

Evan's forehead creases as he processes that. I don't know what else to say. I drove them away. They don't even know I'm sober, I was so embarrassed to be such a disgrace.

Our food arrives, and Evan grins approvingly. A whiff of extreme spice hits me, and I raise an eyebrow at Evan's plate. The fish tacos look delicious, but they're *spilling* over with jalapenos. I thank the waiter and take a bite of my crabcakes: they're silky on the inside, crispy outside, and the flavor has just a bit of heat and a bit of garlic with a strong aroma of citrus. Delicious.

Evan scoops up a fish taco and dunks it into the hot chili sauce, and then into a green sauce I assume is the wasabi. He grabs a few jalapenos from his plate and piles them right onto the sauced bit, and then takes a giant bite. I watch, waiting to see if he'll light on fire or tap out, but he closes his eyes and groans with pleasure.

Yep, the man is a thrill-seeker. I giggle as he washes the bite down with a swig of his whiskey.

"Oh, yeah," he says. "That's the stuff right there."

"You're insane and adorable," I say.

"You should try some."

"It actually looks a little bit frightening."

"Frighteningly delicious," he corrects with a wicked smirk.

I can't resist him. I take a deep breath. He steals the opportunity to snag my fork off my plate and scoop up a little bit of everything: some fish, the toppings, a bit of each sauce, and of course a jalapeno pepper. I'm terrified, but as he holds out the fork and dares me with his eyes, I realize I'd eat a fucking pinecone off a fork if he looked at me like that while he offered it to me. I swallow my fear and dive in.

Holy shit. I'm out of wine, and my mouth is on fire. The flavors are wonderful, but it's all overwhelmed by the heat. I grab Evan's whiskey and take a drink to wash some of the heat out of my mouth, and then follow it with a bite of my own food to distract my taste buds. Evan chuckles, but he looks genuinely concerned beneath his humor.

"It's good, but I stand by my judgement that you are insane."

He purses his lips, displeased with himself. "I wondered if the wasabi might push you a bit far."

I let out a giggle. "I think, Evan, that just about everything with you pushes me a bit far." His frown deepens, so I reach across the table and take his hand. "And I like it. You challenge me."

"So I'm still insane *and* adorable?"

I squeeze his hand, and he eagerly squeezes it back. "Even more so when you're worried about it."

Relief washes over his features, and he calls for the waiter to get me some more wine. He tells me about the time his younger brother challenged him to a habanero pepper eating contest. Evan won, eating three whole, raw peppers before he couldn't eat any more, and his brother, Mickey, only managed two.

"It's still way more than I could eat," I say as I finish my crabcakes.

Evan dunks a jalapeno in the hot sauce and eats it plain. "And I still think I could do better."

Bared

I don't order dessert. Evan talks about work, and I cling to his every word even though I don't understand half of it. Derek's paid Evan really well for both the under-the-hood stuff on his truck as well as the custom exterior, I gather. I don't really listen to the details. I watch his mouth move as he talks. The way he looks at me while he speaks is intoxicating. Like he's not actually talking about a set of rims, but about the way he'd like to lay me down and penetrate me until I can't breathe. I get a little tipsy off my three glasses of wine, and Evan holds my hand as I rise from the table. I slip my arm through the crook of his elbow and snuggle close to him as he leads me to the front desk. I love his smell, the cool feel of his leather, and the strength of his solid body.

I fish out my cell phone as Evan registers a room in his name. I punch in a quick text to Andee, letting her know I'll be home tomorrow. She replies *LOL drunky mcdrunkface, have fun. DETAILS!*

I glance back at my own text, and sure enough I've spelled three words wrong. I don't care. I power the thing down and stuff it back into my purse. There will be no interruptions tonight. No fear of being caught. And I might just get away with pretending I was too drunk to remember the details to spare myself the discomfort of spilling it all to Andee.

Our room is up the winding staircase. I slide my hand along the railing, admiring the cool, smooth wood as we climb, and Evan never lets go of me. He's cool, collected, not rushed. Always eager, but never rushed. I think it's what I like most about him: he experiences every moment to the fullest. I wonder if his father is this way, or if his brother is the same. I've never met anyone like him, and I've met a hell of a lot of people.

Evan hands me the keycard. "After you," he murmurs in my ear. The touch of his lips on my cheek sends electricity shooting through me. Oh, God, I can't wait for this.

The room is elegant with dark wood furniture and pink rose accents. I've spent so long bouncing between home, where I barely keep my head screwed on straight and The Core, where it's too dark for me to see the details of anyone I meet, that this feels like another world. Here, in The Hideaway nestled into the mountains, I'm romanced away from real life and stresses, like I've stepped into the pages of a fantasy story and never have to go back. I run my fingertips along the polished surface of the dresser and glance at the drawers. No locked drawers full of pills harbor my secrets, here. I really am just Alice, the girl Evan wants. I don't have to be the fuckup—who barely keeps her head above water—tonight.

Evan takes off his leather jacket and his shoes and regards me with his head tilted. Then, a boyish grin breaks across his face and he rushes past me, springing into the air and throwing himself face-first onto the lush mattress and pile of pillows.

I burst into laughter, slip off my heels, and join him, jumping onto my back in the giant bed. Evan grabs me as soon as I do, rolling me on top of him and threading his fingers into my hair. His eyes are alight with happiness, and he pulls me down to kiss him. I close my eyes, flicking my tongue along the edge of his lip, and he groans.

"Evan, I have to tell you something," I say.

"Good," he replies, running his thumbs over my cheeks. "I love it when you tell me things."

I swallow hard, gather my nerves. "I really, *really* like you."

He grins, kissing me once.

"It's a problem," I say. "I want to do this again. Go out with you, do exciting things with you. But my job..."

"Don't even worry about that," Evan says. "Why would you worry about that?"

I sigh. "I *have* to flirt. You're not the only one I've fucked on the job. I know that makes me sound like a whore..."

He silences me with a finger to my lips. "Stop it, Alice. Don't talk about yourself that way. I *know* it's your job. I care about you anyway. Hell, I fell for you when you were trying to set me up with someone else. I don't want to change you. I have never wanted to change you. I just want to be in your life, whatever way you'll let me."

Wow. I'm so floored I don't know what to say. Through all his intensity, he's the most open-minded, accepting man. He wants to be with me but not restrict me.

"So... you don't want my exclusivity?" I ask. It stings a little bit to say. I *want* him to want that with me, even though I can't give it to him. I am a whole new level of fucked up and selfish.

Evan laughs. "Hell yeah, I do. But not until you're ready to give it to me. Until then, I can just take you any way I can get you."

It's official: Evan is perfect. Part of me is afraid I'm being heinously unfair to him by leading him on... I'm not going to quit my job, so I don't know when or if I'll ever be ready to give him that exclusivity. But the bigger part of me—screaming at me in my head—appreciates his unconditional acceptance so strongly I don't want to wait another second before I thank him for it. I bite my lip and grab the hem of my shirt, stripping it off over my head.

Evan sucks in a breath and sits up with me, letting his hands glide up my waist to my back. His part, expectant, as he flips open the clasp on my bra, and he slides the straps slowly over my shoulders, never tearing his gaze from mine. I'm exposed astride his lap, and he doesn't reach up to grab my breasts as I expect him to. Instead, he wraps his arms around my waist and crushes me to him, burying his mouth in the crook of my neck. His breath washes hotly over my skin, and I rake my fingernails through his short hair as he hardens beneath me.

"Your turn," I whisper, my hands wandering down to find the hem of his shirt. He pulls back an inch to meet my eyes, and the intensity in his glare has darkened, somehow. My heart kicks into a sprint: what's wrong?

I work the hem of his shirt up over his abs. "Is this okay?" I ask. I don't know why I'm suddenly so nervous. I've wanted nothing more than to see him bare, to taste all of his skin, to feel his warmth along my whole body.

Evan searches my eyes for a moment, his forehead creased with severity, and then nods once. I pull the shirt up and he lifts his arms, letting me peel it off over his head. I toss it aside and admire him: his chest is rock-hard and sculpted like a statue, his abs defined and heaving with every breath. I run my hand down over his chest and grin at him, but he doesn't return the smile. That severity hasn't left his eyes.

"Did I do something wrong?" I ask, my voice a notch higher than usual with fear.

Evan shakes his head and parts his lips as if to speak, but nothing comes out.

"Evan, what is it?"

He blinks, *finally*, and runs his hands across my lower back again. He pulls me to him, and the warmth of his chest

74

pressed against my breasts sends a thrill of arousal through me. I rock against him and slide my hands around his waist, too.

A ridge on his skin steals my attention. Evan stills instantly, not breathing, and I'm not sure I know how to breathe, either. I trace the ridge all the way up to the top of his right shoulder, across his upper back to the other shoulder, and then down across his back in a harsh diagonal. A scar? I open my eyes and try to process what I'm seeing. A massive, triangular scar mars the skin of Evan's back from top to bottom.

I lick my lips, and my voice comes out in a scrape of shock. "What happened?"

Evan doesn't let go of me, but he shakes a little bit as he draws a breath to speak. "Road rash. I was hit on my bike... my old bike. Busted my leg in two places, wrecked my back, and cut my head really good, too."

The skin of the scar is darker than the rest of his back, and the raised edges of it are a deep, purplish pink. A sick, nagging feeling that I should pull my hand away eats at me, but I can't bring myself to move. I don't know what to say, or if I should say anything at all.

"I'm lucky I lived," Evan says, his voice even darker than before. "Most people don't survive that level of trauma. It was a major skin graft. I was on a ventilator for three weeks— two of my ribs perforated my lungs—and in the hospital for five months."

Jesus. Christ. I can't picture Evan like that, the spark silenced as a machine breathes for him in paper gowns and curtains. All this time I've viewed him as this perfect, carefree man, capable of nothing but adventure and passion. Here I find he's endured a hell I've never imagined. Still, my fucked up mind wanders toward the worst possible thing I could say, and it slips out.

"You don't need pain pills?" *Fucking hell, Alice.* I reason with myself that I only want to make sure I won't ever see him take them and be tempted, but deep down in the pit of my stomach, I know the truth: I want to know if he got hooked on them, too. I could maybe tell him, if he did. He'd understand.

"Nah," Evan says, both relieving my stress and tripling it at the same time. "I never took them once I was out of the hospital. They insisted when I was in there, but I didn't bother to fill the prescription after. It was hard enough for Dad without me being out of it mentally, as well as physically. Mom died only a few years before." His tone darkens again.

This is the first time Evan's gone more than thirty seconds without looking at me, so I pull back and meet his eyes. He seems apologetic, like he's still sorry he put his dad through it all... or maybe he's afraid he's wrecked my view of his perfection. He couldn't be more wrong.

"That's why you live like you're dying," I whisper.

He nods. "I'll never do anything half-assed. It can all fall apart so quickly. Any day could be our last together."

He's right. It all makes sense: why he approached me with such passion and insistence, why he takes every opportunity for excitement to the fullest extreme. Why his eyes light with anxiety every time I pull away. "I don't know what to say. I didn't realize..."

That intensity I adore flares. "Just don't say you would have done things differently had you known. Don't say you don't want me because of this. I know it's ugly... you don't have to look at it. At least my hair hides the worst of it on my head."

I shake my head, desperate to soothe him. "Evan, not at all. Not even close. I want you. You don't have any reason to hide from me."

He swallows hard and takes my face between his palms. "Then don't hide from *me,* Alice. There's something you're not telling me, something you *want* to tell me. What is it?"

Am I that transparent? My mouth goes dry. "Some scars are worn on the inside, I guess." Lame, Alice. Fucking lame.

Evan grinds his teeth together and threads his hands back into my hair. "You know what I think?"

"What do you think?" My voice is barely a whisper above the pounding of my heart.

"I think you hold yourself to a higher standard than everyone else around you. You want me even though I'm brutally scarred? Well, I'll love you if you're scarred, too. No matter how ugly it is, you're beautiful to me."

My mind sticks on that word. Love. Does Evan love me? He can't. He loves an illusion of me, the perfection I put forth to hide my true self. A sickness rolls through me at my own omission, but my heart clenches at his words, and I don't want to wait a second longer. I throw my arms around him and kiss him, letting my hands stroke down his back over his scars. He squeezes me against him, my nipples perking as his muscles tense, and we're right back where we were before I discovered his scars. They don't change how much I want him, and I rock my hips forward, pressing on his hardness until he loses his breath. Evan flips me onto my back and climbs between my legs.

"You like it when I push you?" he says, reminding me of our conversation at dinner.

"God, yes."

He grabs my wrists and pulls my arms up above my head, pinning them down against the pillow.

"Do you want me to push you here, too?" he asks, his voice rough with desire as he grips me tight. "I've held back. I didn't want to scare you off. You think I live like I'm dying?

You want to see how I'd do things with you if this really was our last day together?"

My mouth goes dry again. I have no idea what that means. But I don't want to waste a moment with Evan. His passion has already swept me off my feet. If he knows how to take it further... if he has been holding back... I want every drop of him I can get no matter what it involves.

"Yes, Evan," I say. "Push me."

His eyes flare with savage desire, and he presses down against me, jamming his hips against mine. I cry out at the sensation.

"Okay, Alice," he says, his lips hovering over mine. "Hang on tight."

Pushed

Evan doesn't hesitate. He seizes my mouth, kissing me until I'm writhing against him, begging for more. I need his touch. I *need* his body. I reach down to his jeans and grasp at the button, but he restrains my wrist and pins my hands above my head.

"Stop trying to control it," Evan murmurs, his lips hovering over mine so close they brush against me when he speaks. "That's my job."

I whimper, pull against him once, but he doesn't let me go.

"Shh," he says. He squeezes my wrist once. I love the possession of his touch. I can't get enough of it, and I pull against him again just so he'll clench me tighter. His arms bulge as he pins me there. God, he's perfect. How could he think that I'd be turned off by his scars? His body is beautiful, and the scars tell the story of how he came to be the amazing, passionate, driven man he is.

I let go. Stop resisting his control. He kisses down my neck to my breasts and takes my nipple in his mouth, sucking briefly while he still restrains my wrist on the pillow. His other hand works down my side, grasping at me, stroking my skin, and his palm comes to rest on my hip. He rocks against me once more, his hardness obvious even through his jeans. He wants me as badly as I want him.

"Evan," I whisper.

"Yes, Alice?" he pulls back and peers at me with humor in his eyes.

"I need you," I say. "I need this."

He chuckles and kisses me slowly on the lips. "You got it, baby."

Evan releases my hand and within seconds my skirt is gone from my hips. My panties follow, flung across the room by a man so hungry for me it takes my breath away. He straightens on his knees above me and unzips his jeans, and I pant on the bed, naked and begging for his touch to return to my skin. He peels off his jeans slowly, his erection jumping free of his boxers, and then pauses, staring but not yet climbing between my legs.

"My God, you're beautiful," he says, wrapping his hand around his long, thick shaft. My toes curl at his words, and the air in the room chills my body, my nipples perking under his glare.

He strokes his hand up and down his shaft. "I could look at you all day."

"Evan," I plead.

"Let me look at you," he says, his eyes so heated I can feel his gaze warming my skin every inch it travels. He tilts his head, studying my breasts, the curve of my waist, and then my hips. His hand moves quicker as his glare settles between my legs, and his breath quickens.

I can feel him fucking me with his eyes. Fire ignites inside me and I want him to drive into me *right now*. Instead, he lowers himself down onto his side, parts my legs with his free hand, and dives forth to capture me in his mouth once more.

I cry out, my head tossing back on the pillow. He knows what he's doing with his mouth, that's for damn sure. His tongue strokes over the sensitive bud, never too rough, never too fast. He groans at the taste of me, his hand still moving over his cock while he licks. I reach down and let my fingertips glide through his hair, and then I rub the top of his shoulders. He stills when I touch his scar, but then squeezes his eyes shut, licking long, agonizingly perfect strokes as I run my hands along his back.

Pleasure builds inside me. It's so fast, this time. Automatic. My body reacts to the way I feel about Evan before he really gets going. My muscles clench, goose bumps running over my skin.

"Evan," I gasp, "Evan, I'm close."

He snaps his head up and climbs over me. "No, you don't," he growls. "Not without me inside you."

He drives his hips forward. I'm so wet; he slides all the way into me in one long, smooth thrust, filling me. I shriek at the sensation, and he starts moving, fast. Heat rushes through my center, and I cry out with every thrust. His hot, muscled chest presses down against mine as he wraps me in his arms, one hand sprawled across my lower back, the other on my backside, squeezing. He clutches me against his body, and I can hardly breathe with the hard, fast thrusts of his length into me.

"Evan," I manage, but I'm too close to say more. I suck in a breath, hold it, and he bites my neck. The sensation spears straight through my core, mixing the hot pleasure of his lips and tongue with just a glint of pain, and I lose it. I crash around him, my hips bucking up into his thrusts, his shaft thickening inside me every time I convulse.

"Yes, Alice," Evan growls. "Oh, yes, more!"

I can't think. He grinds into me harder, alternating between pressing into the back of me, no space between us, and pounding fast, his length pushing me open with each thrust. I dig my fingertips into his biceps, my nails biting at his skin, and then I lose it again. The orgasm rushes through me so fast I don't have time to warn him, and he groans loudly with satisfaction as he feels it happen.

"God, Alice, yes," he manages, breathless. "Again. Come again."

I'm still spiraling down from the second orgasm, but he pushes up on his palms, finds my hand with his, and brings it down between us so my fingertips rest just over my clit. I feel my own throbbing, and it's so intimate, so exposed, that I turn my head away, unable to look at him while I touch myself.

"More," Evan demands, capturing my lips with his. "Alice, let me see you." He pulls out to shallower thrusts, his head rubbing that perfect, sensitive spot just a couple inches inside me, so he can look down and watch what I'm doing.

Shyness threatens behind my arousal, and I almost stop the motion of my hand. But Evan's expression—his eyebrows knitted as his gaze rakes over my body—tells me this is what he wants to see. He wants to watch me touch myself, wants to see me unravel all over again. Desire sparks inside me, hotter with desperation: I want to show him this. To give him this, to live like I'm dying *with* him. I don't want to miss a moment of what we have together out of shyness or anything else.

I move my fingertips in a circle, and Evan lets out a loud, satisfied groan. He pumps in and out of me in short strokes, looking between my hand and my eyes. I'm caught in his sights, locked in his spell, and as heat spreads through me once more, my breathing grows shallow and quick. I let my other hand wander over to my nipple, and Evan watches me pinch the tip lightly. I start to move, lifting my hips, wanting more of him inside me, but he just gives me this little bit, just enough that we're connected, yet not so deeply that I can't pleasure myself at the same time.

I watch him as intensely as he watches me. Sweat breaks out on his forehead as he continues his torturous, short thrusts, his jaw clenched tight. He's holding himself back from the edge, I can tell. I quicken the motion of my fingertips, pinch my nipple harder. His glare flashes with urgency, and I close my eyes, willing myself closer.

It builds slowly, and Evan grinds his teeth, holding back as he keeps moving that little bit. I whimper and revel in the delicious torture of it all, the sensitivity inside me increasing with every movement he makes. I let my fingers rub faster, harder, and Evan groans aloud.

"Baby," he pleads. "Come on me. I need it. I need you."

God motherfucking damn yes. "I'm close," I whisper.

His eyes dart up to mine and he licks his lips. "Come on me. Please."

I rub harder. My toes curl again, my back arching off the bed. I'm so close.

"Alice!" His voice is sharp with warning. "Now, Alice!"

He doesn't have to tell me again. I suck in a breath and the orgasm rips through me, blanking my brain. I shriek and the muscles pulse deliciously inside me, and Evan lets out a sharp growl. He buries himself inside me, trapping my hand against myself where I throb as the orgasm spins relentlessly through me. He's hot, heavy, and he bites my neck again. The pinch of his teeth sends a shock through my center and without any warning, I explode all over again, throwing my head back and calling out. Evan presses into the deepest part of me and rides the waves of my orgasm, and then he pushes back, grabs my wrists out from between us and slams my hands above my head. He pins me there and stares into my eyes—into my soul—as he releases, shooting heat into the depths of my body. I rock against him, panting, as the orgasm blasts on and on. We move in rhythm with each other, pulsing, aching, moaning.

We come down slowly from the high. Evan releases my wrists and brings my hands down, gently kissing my still-damp fingertips. He shifts us to our sides, his body still locked inside mine, and curls his arm around my neck so his bicep is my pillow. He smells of cologne and whiskey and sex... delicious. I kiss his chest, nestled so close to his pounding heart as he tries to slow his heavy breathing.

There's no denying it: Evan is amazing. Perfect in every way. That was the most mind-blowing sex of my life. And I've had a lot of sex.

A flash of panic hits me and I jerk my head up. "Evan!" I gasp. "Condom!"

He meets my gaze, pursing his lips. "Shit," he says. "I have one in my jacket."

"It's a little late now," I say. I was so in the moment... I didn't think. That's not like me at all. I'm the damn condom police at The Core. How the hell did I manage to screw this up?

"Yeah, I realize that." He chuckles. "Damn. If I knock you up you're stuck with me forever. What a shame *that* would be." He smirks.

I slap him playfully on the arm. "I'm on the pill. And I wouldn't rope you in like that."

He puts on a pout, still breathing fairly hard. It occurs to me: he really *wouldn't* mind being stuck with me forever. And the longer I spend with him, the more he surprises me and romances me with his seductive words, the clearer this all becomes. I wouldn't mind being stuck with him, either.

"I'm clean," I rush to say. "I know with my job it probably looks like I'm not, but I'm really very careful, and I get tested frequently just to be doubly sure."

He shakes his head. "Stop thinking that I assume the worst about you, Alice. I know you'd have told me if there was something for me to worry about. Like, when I ate you out the other night, for instance." He laughs boyishly at the memory, and I can't help but giggle with him.

"Yeah, I guess that would have been a good time," I say.

"And I haven't been with anyone since my accident, so you're safe, too." He kisses me on the tip of the nose.

Relief presses away my looming worry. The feeling of his heat with no barrier between us was beyond delicious. I snug my leg around his hip to keep him inside as he relaxes.

Evan strokes my hair back from my face. "That was okay? I didn't push you too far?"

I shake my head vigorously. "God, Evan. Do you have any idea how good at this you are? How you pleasure me, how you surprise me?"

A grin of true mirth peels across his lips. "Does that mean you want to go out with me again sometime?"

I can't help but giggle. "Hell yes, I do. All the time, if you don't mind."

He kisses my hair and pulls me closer into his embrace. "I think we can work something out."

Insurance

Morning comes too quickly. Evan and I remain tangled around each other all night long, and when the sun breaks through the pale curtains and we emerge from the dark comfort of sleep, he envelops me in the masterful pleasure of his mouth. There's a serious edge to his kisses, the way he tastes me, the way he holds me close. Like he's afraid now that the night's over, our time together will be, too. Even when he enters me again, hard as rock, he wraps me in his arms and moves slowly, drawing out our union. I'm sore and still pulsing with orgasm when he releases inside me, and he kisses me the whole time we're connected until his breathing slows and he withdraws.

Showering with Evan is an even more intense experience. I get a good look at his scar for the first time, struggling not to show my horror that he was damaged so severely. I want to ask him more about the accident, but I can see the way he tenses when I wash his back and run my soapy hand over the ridges of the scar, so I think better of it. I catch a glimpse of the scar on his head when he's rinsing his hair, and it's huge. At least five inches of gash wrapping around his scalp from behind his temple to the crown of his head. Again I'm hit with a wave of gratitude that Evan survived the wreck. My life would be the same as it was a few weeks ago, if he hadn't.

I've loved my life in The Core, up until this point. I've felt fulfilled and happy. I had no idea what was missing, what could be added to my life, until Evan walked in and shook everything upside down. Nerves bleed into my mood, even as I press my cheek to his chest, his hands holding me by the backside, and the water cascades around us. I don't know what Derek will say when we meet, and I'm terrified to find out. But even if my job falls through and I'm left empty-handed, there's a new point of strength in my life. Leaving The Core wouldn't mean I'd jump right back into addiction and numbing the pain with pills, as I've feared for so long. I'd just have to find another job, and I'd still have Evan.

He takes the ride home slow. Winding down the steep hills is even more exhilarating than climbing up them, and I find myself far less interested in the scenery than I am in the feel of my hands on Evan's abs. Every now and then he glances back in my direction, and then resumes his attention to the road. I didn't think it was possible to dread the end of this date any more than I already do, but every time the miles on the signs we pass indicate we're closer to the city, my heart thumps a little bit harder. I don't want this to be over.

Evan pulls right in front of my apartment building when I point it out, and I climb off the bike. He takes off his helmet and runs a hand through his hair before I hold out my helmet to him.

He frowns at it. "Or you could keep it," he says, "and give it to me next time."

I smirk. "Is that some kind of insurance policy that I'll go out with you again?"

He shrugs innocently, and I can't help but laugh. His insecurity is adorable, and so totally unnecessary.

"Okay, then," I say. "I'll keep it." I hug the helmet close.

He grins and pulls me forward by my hand. I kiss him deeply, reveling in the taste of his breath, all the memories that surge forth when his lips touch me. What a surprising, perfect night. What an unexpected, amazing man.

"Call me," I whisper when we break the kiss.

"I will. I'll harass the shit out of you until we go out again."

I know he's telling me the truth, and my heart breaks into a sprint as he says it. I can't fucking wait.

He slips his helmet back on and waits to tear down the street until I'm through the security doors of my building. I glance back. He looks fucking sexy as hell as he rides, leaned back in the seat. I let myself in upstairs. Andee whirls in her chair at the computer where she often sits to work on school stuff, jumping to her feet.

"Details!" she shrieks. "I'm dying over here! Evan is fucking *gorgeous,* Alice, are you two like, together now? Like for real together? Tell me you're together!"

I put my hands on her shoulders to slow her bouncing and giggle at her excitement. "Yes, Andee. I think so."

She grabs my shoulders, too, and before I know it, we're doing that annoying girl thing, jumping up and down together and squealing. I don't even mind.

We drop onto the couch and Andee tucks her legs up beneath herself. I tell her all about the ride, the Hideaway, and even a little bit about the sex. "Four damn times. I'm not kidding. I almost got sick of orgasms."

"How can you get sick of orgasms?" She snorts.

"You can't, that's why I said *almost.*"

"When are you going to see him again?" Andee hangs onto every word I say.

I sigh. "I don't know. I have to meet with Derek tomorrow, so I don't know how that's going to pan out." Those nerves pick back up again. Yes, I'd be fine without The Core, but I don't *want* to have to try it out. I love that place.

Andee's smile falls. "Okay. Listen, Alice, Derek made me swear our conversation was confidential, so you have to pretend I didn't tell you this."

Stress kicks into high gear. "Tell me what?"

She sighs, rests her hand on my knee. "He called me yesterday. Asked me some weird questions."

"Like what?" Waiting is killing me.

"Like... how I feel I'm doing, and whether I think I'm ready to step into a management position. I'd still have the matchmaking duties, but I'd be able to run the place myself, and I'd have a key."

My heart sinks. Drops through the floor and lands on the head of the tenant who lives below us. "Oh. What did you say?"

Andee swallows hard. "I didn't know what to say. That's *your* promotion, and you deserve it. So I said that, and he told me what he does with you isn't really my business."

I can't believe this. Derek cares about me. He always has. Now he's giving Andee my promotion?

"You deserve it too, Andee," I manage, but my heart isn't in the words. It's still thumping way down below where the tenant beneath us is probably scooping it up with a broom.

She looks down at her fingers. "I'm sorry. I told him if he gives me the position I'll happily accept it, but that I'm not comfortable doing anything until you're aware of what's going on. This is all so out-of-the-blue, and I have no idea what he's thinking."

"Me either." I'm growing more afraid of tomorrow with each moment that passes. I can handle getting fired. But getting the verbal disappointment from Derek is going to sting like hell.

"Alice, does Derek know about you and Evan?"

I shrug. "Yeah, he knows. What does that have to do with anything?"

Andee stills and then she takes my hand. "Have you ever wondered if he has feelings for you that are deeper than just the boss-employee relationship?"

I don't know what to make of that. "You know Derek and I fucked. A lot. He's the one who taught me how to break my addiction to instant gratification. He saved me, in so many ways."

"And now that you're *ready* to date, do you think maybe he wishes you picked him?"

"He would have asked me long ago." My voice is hollow. Derek has watched over me so protectively over the last few years. Protectively... or possessively? My head spins.

Andee squeezes my hand. "You know what, I'm probably just imagining this. If Derek is giving me a promotion, I'm sure he's giving you one, too. Maybe he wants us to manage together and that way he gets more time off, you know?"

"Yeah, maybe." My chest hurts from anxiety. My mind flits over a memory of the pleasant, numbing sensation that ripples over me like a warm bath when a pill dissolves in my stomach, and I press the thought away. I will *not* resort to old habits when the tiniest bit of stress hits.

"Listen, Andee, I'm pretty tired from the night, obviously. I'm gonna catch up on some sleep."

She pats my leg and stands. "Okay. Just let me know if you need anything. Wanna do pizza tonight?"

"Sure." I move to my bedroom as Andee resumes her attention to her schoolwork.

I sit on my bed. It's cold when I stretch out beneath the blankets. I can't even begin to imagine how my conversation with Derek tomorrow might go. I crave numbness more and more with every minute that passes, and I find myself curled up in a ball, clutching my head. I will not give in. I will *not* go get those pills.

Instead, I let my mind wander toward Evan. I think about his hands, his mouth, his scarred back. The memory of his body, heavy and sweating against mine, helps soothe some of the fear. I imagine his mouth on my neck, biting like he does, and his arms wrapped around me.

I imagine telling him the words I don't know how to spit out, and him telling me he loves me, too.

Face It Head-On

I wait outside The Core with that nervous pang twisting in my chest. Andee's words have been brewing in my mind since she said them yesterday. I didn't manage more than one slice of pizza and maybe an hour and a half of sleep, and though Andee offered me a drink to calm down, I had to refuse it. If I started numbing the nervous edge away, even with alcohol, I might slip closer to those old habits.

I dig the toe of my shoe against a discarded cigarette butt, trying to smash it into nothingness, but all I manage to do is squeeze out the last bit of tobacco and make a mess. I let out a sigh and scoop it up, tossing it in the trash near the door. A truck roars around the corner, but it's white, not Derek's signature black. My heart is pounding. I'm so scared of what's coming. If he fires me and I have to clean out my dressing room, will I manage to throw that bag of pills in the trash on my way out?

No. I won't. I don't know how to deal with pain. I fish my phone out of my purse and glance through the texts... Evan's promise to pick me up on Sunday after I've slept off the Saturday night shift at The Core, and Andee's wish for good luck. I'll cling to this, if it all goes sour. I'll hang onto their friendship, their words, the care they have for me. They'd hate me if they found me curled up in a pile of barf, half-conscious from a handful of oxy.

Yet even as I cling to the comfort of the two people who are waiting to hear how it goes, I count pills in my head. One pill in every bottle in that bag occupying my locked drawer. I have at least seven pure oxy, a few blended painkillers with oxy, and twelve pills with some form of codeine. Plenty to last me a week if I take them one at a time. Which I won't. Shit. Maybe it'll be enough to take the edge off my shame for a few days just until I get my feet under me again.

I try the door handle again, even though I know Derek's not here yet. I can't stand the waiting. I just want this over with. If I'm right and I'm fired, I've gotta keep my head screwed on straight. If Andee's right and Derek has feelings for me beyond our professional relationship, I'll have to screw his head on straight. Which means rejecting him, and probably getting fired anyway. It's not that I don't have feelings for him, too, on some level. It's just that Evan is... well, he's Evan. And I'm pretty damn sure he's meant for me.

Another engine rumbles down the street, and I stiffen, sickness rolling all the way through my insides. It's him. The black truck parks illegally right outside the entrance, and Derek steps out. He comes around the front of his truck, looking as sexy as he always does in a black t-shirt and jeans. His dark skin is an even deeper tone than usual. He must have gotten some sun over the last few days.

"Ready?" he asks me.

I nod, but can't meet his chocolate eyes. He pauses in his stride and lets out a sigh. His finger touches my chin and I look up.

"Try to relax, Alice. We're just having a meeting."

Fuck, fuck, fuck. I'm as transparent as glass. "You're firing me, aren't you?" I blurt out.

Derek's eyes tense, and he pulls his hand away. The heartbeats tick by as he considers it.

"Let's talk in my office," he says.

I swallow hard as he opens the door, and then I follow him inside.

We move beyond the bar and the booths and the DJ booth and the spiral staircase leading upstairs. God, I love this place. I'm on the verge of tears already and nothing's even happened yet. This place is my home, my sanctuary. I don't know how I'm going to live without it.

Numbness creeps into my thoughts, and I shake it away. I let Evan's pure, green eyes flash into my head instead, replacing the desire for drugs with the desire for his body. Inside me, around me, any way I can get him.

By the time we reach Derek's office at the end of the corridor behind the hidden curtain, my eyes are dry and I'm holding my head high. He sits at his desk, and I steal a glance at the cracked-open door leading to his secondary office, which is really more like an apartment suite. I've been in there with him so many times, when I was still the broken junkie with no self-control at all. In the bed, in the shower, on the floor. I loved every moment of it with him. It taught me to enjoy the wait, to be patient, to break my addiction to instant-gratification. As I take in the sight of his sculpted forearms, leaning on his desk, I swallow hard. I could have fallen for Derek, had I not kept romance so adamantly out of my mind until Evan rocked my world.

"Stop panicking," Derek scolds me, his voice stern. "If we're gonna get through this, you've gotta keep yourself together. Breathe, Alice."

I do as he says. Derek knows me better than anyone. Better than Andee, better than Evan.

"Why do you think I would fire you?"

I clear my throat and force my voice out. "My performance has been shit."

"How so?"

Why can't he just get it over with? "Come on, Derek, don't do the typical-boss-performance-evaluation shit with me. Just give it to me straight."

He sits back, his hands folded in his lap. "That's not the kind of patience I taught you."

I scoff. "If you're firing me, everything you've taught me has been for nothing anyway. So get on with it."

"Alice," Derek snaps, "it is in your best interest to cooperate with me right now. Tell me: how do you feel your performance has been shit?"

I want to crawl into a hole in the floor and vanish. I thumb my phone, reminding myself I'm valued by more than just Derek, and this isn't the end of the world no matter what happens.

"Andee and I got drunk with those two rich guys last week. And I haven't been as attentive as I should have been on the dance floor my last two shifts. I miscalculated how much rum we've gone through on the inventory—you caught that one—and I don't spend as much time on the rooftop as Andee does."

Derek frowns. "That's why there are two matchmakers though, isn't it? Why I hired Andee? To help you balance it all out."

"You hired Andee because she's a vixen in the sack," I retort.

Derek shoots daggers at me. "Don't you *dare* accuse me of that," he growls. "Have I not always been fair with you? I have never expected you or anyone else to sleep with me before or during employment. You know better than this, Alice, and frankly, I don't deserve bullshit accusations like that from anyone. Especially not from you."

I shrink. He's right. Andee was the one who approached *Derek* for sex. He didn't require it of her or of me. Hell, I wasn't even looking for a job when I slept with him. I just wanted something to take my mind off the withdrawals, and he did the trick.

"I'm sorry," I manage. "I don't know what's gotten into me."

"Evan's gotten into you," he says.

My heart stalls. Oh fucking shit. Andee was right. This isn't about my performance. This is about Evan. Or maybe it's about Derek and me. And the more I remember our time together, the way he helped and healed me and then gave me a shot at a new life here, the more I realize how unfair I've been to him. I haven't given anyone a chance since I got clean, and now I'm giving Derek's chance to Evan.

I peer up at him, my eyelashes heavy with moisture. I swore I wouldn't cry in front of Derek. I swore it.

"Alice," Derek murmurs, his voice gentler now, "are you okay? You've been seeing him a lot. It's not like you."

"I'm okay." My voice sounds hollow, far away. Like I'm not sure who I am, or what I'm doing anymore.

"Why are you crying?"

I dash the tears away with the back of my hand. "I don't know, Derek. I'm so sorry."

"What are you sorry for, Alice?" His gentle voice lures me to him. I've always cherished the way he says my name, the way he treats it with care. And now I'm going to crush him, and I hate myself for it.

I take a deep breath and meet his chocolate eyes. "I love him, Derek. I'm in love with Evan."

Derek's eyes shift between mine, and my heart pounds so hard it mimics the bass from the speakers when The Core is alive with sweaty patrons, booze, dancing, and sex. He licks his lips and draws a slow breath.

96

"Well, then," he says. "Let's do this." He reaches into his desk and pulls out a folder full of papers. Is that my file? Oh, fuck.

I wish he'd just rip off the band-aid. Stop playing games and fire my ass now so I can leave in private shame. But because he's Derek, he's going to draw this out. He draws everything out.

But he doesn't pull out a pink slip. He pulls out a big, folded piece of blue paper and starts opening it up. It's huge, and covers almost his entire desk. What the hell is this?

I lean forward. It's a blueprint. I don't know how to read it, but before I get a chance to ask, Derek pulls a rolled tube from under his desk. He pops it open and spreads it out on top of the blueprint, and my jaw falls open. It's a sketch of a building. A tall, brightly-lit building with a red carpet out front and revolving glass doors. The name of the place is sketched and filled in with red marker to give the illusion of a lit sign.

"What is this?" I ask.

Derek flashes me a giddy, eager grin. "It's my new club downtown. The Haven."

I shake my head, wordless. Why is he showing me this?

"Andee is going to manage The Core while you and I are getting it all running. But I want to focus on marketing, not design. So The Haven is yours, Alice. You'll design the interior to suit your vision for a place like The Core, and you'll run it on your own. I'm just the background guy... the owner, investor, whatever. The big shot in a suit, without the suit."

I hold up a hand, stunned. "Wait, stop," I say. "I'm not fired?"

Derek laughs. "Alice, do you know how overjoyed I am that you're finally letting go of your old bullshit and living your life? You're in love. You're happy. You're ready for this."

My heart clenches. Derek's giving me a club to run. How can he be so good to me? My head is spinning and I can't draw a breath.

"Say something, Alice," Derek urges.

"Thank you?" I manage.

He laughs and reaches out to take my hand. "You're welcome. You have worked hard and deserve this. But be ready to work even harder, now."

"I will," I choke out. "I don't know what to say."

He winks at me. "Go tell Andee and Evan. They're probably dying waiting, right now."

I spring to my feet and turn around without a word. I've gotta tell them! Holy fucking shit, I'm going to be running The Haven! A brand new club like this one, but custom designed how I want it. How do I want it? I can't form a coherent thought.

"Alice," Derek calls at my back.

I face him, still speechless.

"Party at my place tonight. I'm shutting The Core down for the evening so we can celebrate. Make sure you bring a date."

I blink rapidly at him. A party at Derek's house. He not only supports my career, but my relationship with Evan. Even the fact that I'm in love with him.

I don't know what I did to deserve Derek or Evan or Andee, but I'm not going to jinx it. I break into a grin, rush forward, and throw myself into Derek's arms, hugging him, thanking him. He laughs into my hair. When he releases me, those tears are on my cheeks again, and this time, I don't mind at all.

I've gotta tell Evan. He'll be so happy for me, and Andee will be so relieved. And maybe I can muster up the courage to say those three little words to Evan that I'm dying to say.

Never Hold Back

My hands don't stop shaking for the whole drive back to my apartment. I park my SUV in the garage and make my way up the stairs, still bewildered. Andee springs up from her computer chair when I step through the door, and somehow I manage to spit the words out through my giddy, excited mood.

"Andee," I say, "I'm not fired."

"Thank fucking God," she says, her hand to her heart. "What's this all about, then?"

I wring my fingers together for a moment, forming the words in my head, and then meet her expectant eyes. "The Haven. Derek's new club downtown. It's mine."

Her mouth drops open. "Yours? Like *yours* yours?"

"I get to design it and run it. I'm Derek's partner." I can hardly believe it still.

And then we're doing that damn girl thing again, squealing and jumping up and down. I throw my arms around Andee's neck and hug her tight, telling her how I wouldn't be here without her. I was good at my job before Andee showed up, sure. But she's my best friend, my supporter, my everything, too.

I text Evan as we're getting changed for the evening. He agrees to meet me at Derek's house for a party, and thankfully, already knows where it is. I'm too excited to figure out how to give him directions from Meyer's. I let my hair down. Curl it into a messy style that will bounce when I walk, and can't stop grinning like an idiot in the mirror as I stroke on some eye shadow and mascara.

Andee drives to Derek's. I don't trust myself behind the wheel tonight. My knees shake like hell as we pull up in front of his massive, white house, flanked with brightly lit paths and expensive flowerbeds. When Andee kills the engine of her little car and the bass of the party inside seeps in through the windows, I turn to her.

"Is my outfit too much for Derek's *house*?" I ask.

She laughs as if I've said the most ridiculous thing. "Hell no! You look fucking hot!"

I'm barely wearing anything. Just a bikini top, a skirt so short it hardly counts as more than underwear, a white jacket with a faux-fur trim and piles of long necklaces and beaded bracelets. But Andee's right. It's one of my most daring looks that earns me the most attention at The Core, so I give Andee an appreciative grin and slip out of the car.

I'm greeted by huge smiles from all the regular employees and supporters of The Core. Derek grabs me into a bear hug and I get fist-bumps from the security guys hanging out in the entryway, and then I follow Andee as she almost skips out into the vast backyard, which is decorated with strings of little white lights. The music pounds, our DJ set up in a booth near the balcony, where the waitresses of The Core have gathered and are mingling with the other guests. I'm too nervous to count heads, but I'm pretty sure there's over fifty people spread out across Derek's backyard, including some of our wealthiest patrons like Christopher. He lingers in a corner, very obviously putting the moves on one of the waitresses, who eats up the attention with eagerness. I make my way over to the bar with Andee. She orders herself a vodka slime and cocks an eyebrow at me, but I shake my head discreetly and she just gets me a Coke. If I start drinking now, I won't stop until I'm too wasted to stand.

A warm hand rests on my bare, lower back as I'm leaning against the bar with Andee, and I turn to meet Evan's perfect, green gaze. He pulls me close and I kiss him deeply, unafraid to show him affection in front of all these people. Andee clears her throat and makes her way over to Derek, so I break the kiss and smile at Evan.

"How was your day?" I ask him.

"It was fine, but it's just got a hell of a lot better now that I'm with you," he replies with a smirk. He glances around the yard. "What's all this for? I thought you had a meeting today."

"We shut down for a special occasion. You'll see."

He glares playfully at me. "I'm dying to know, Alice."

"I know."

The music quiets, and Derek hops up on a table beside the DJ booth and calls for everyone's attention. Evan and I turn, and he drapes himself around me from behind, his strong arms locked around my waist.

"I'm not gonna bore you all with a long speech," he booms across the yard, "but thank you all for coming. It is my great pleasure to announce that the lovely matchmaker Andee..." he gestures to my best friend, "...has been promoted to manager of The Core!"

There are claps and whistles, but a few uneasy eyes shift around, pointedly avoiding me. *They think Derek gave her my job.* I cup my hands around my mouth and hoot and holler for Andee's success, and more voices join me until the yard is roaring with congratulations, and Andee gives a little curtsey of thanks.

"One more thing," Derek says, holding up a finger, and I can't help but giggle. "Alice, get your ass up here."

I do, taking his hand as he hoists me up to stand on top of the table, balancing carefully in my heels. I get a few wolf-whistles, and Derek puts his arm around my shoulders.

"You all know Alice. I'm sure she's helped you whenever you needed it, and gotten you laid at least a handful of times."

I stick horns in the air with my hands, and get a round of applause. My face burns red, but this attention feels good. I have busted my ass. I have earned this.

"Alice is one of the best things I've ever brought to The Core. She's more than just an incredible matchmaker. She's my right hand and my friend. It is my deepest honor to announce that I've acquired a new nightclub downtown, and Alice is my partner in both ownership and management of the place. The Core will carry on as it always has, but Alice has a vision for the new club. Alice, why don't you tell us about it?"

The blood drains from my face as he puts me on the spot. I haven't even had time to catch my breath, let alone plan out the place. Murmurs of excitement ripple through the crowd, and I glance over them all, silent. And then my eyes settle on Evan's encouraging grin, and I know what to say. I take a deep breath, flash him a smile in return, and it all just comes to me.

"The Core has brought singles together for everything they've ever wanted. I've had so many unforgettable nights there. It's become a home, and you're all like my family. Our new club is called The Haven, and it's going to strengthen those bonds for every person who walks through the door. The Haven is a place for couples to come and mingle with other couples, with all the freedoms and fun of The Core, but for those who are looking to reconnect with their partner, or explore connecting in new ways, with new people." My eyes settle back on Evan. "Or just to strengthen the connection they already feel... the bonds that are so strong no one can shake them. I am so excited to work with Derek on this project, and thank you—all of you—for making The Core a home so perfect I never could have dreamed it up." Those tears that have been looming prick behind my eyelids, and I shake my head to clear it, earning another round of cheers from the crowd.

"Okay, Alice, you'll put them to sleep before the party even starts," Derek teases, and I laugh. "Drinks all you want, it's all on me, but don't break my shit. Thanks for coming!"

The party erupts into motion as the DJ hits the music again, and Derek helps me down from the table before giving me another hug. Evan strolls over and gives Andee a quick peck on the cheek before pulling back and shouting his congratulations for both of us. Christopher sweeps in and grabs Andee, tugging her off for a celebratory dance, and I fold my fingers around Evan's hand.

"Should we go somewhere quiet?" I say.

He eyes me up and down, and then purses his lips. "Does the guest of honor have to stay all night? I'm dying to strip parts of that outfit off you and see the rest of your beautiful skin."

My cheeks heat as he looks at me like that. My panties don't stand a chance of lasting the night dry if he keeps undressing me with those green eyes. "I think I can duck out early. I need to mingle a bit, but then we can take off if you want."

He catches his lip between his teeth as he glances over my body again. "Did you bring your helmet?"

Desire pulls inside me. "It's in Andee's car."

The music lures us to the center of the party, and I share a couple dances with Andee, earning the attention of everybody in the yard. Later I find Derek and give him a long, heartfelt hug. He tells me he'll make sure Andee gets home safely with an approving wink. Evan and I slip out and he walks me to Andee's car where I retrieve his spare helmet.

"I never go out without my insurance," I say.

Evan takes my hand. "Good." We hop onto his bike. He peels out into the night, and the wind is cool on my bare skin, but he takes it slow since I'm barely dressed. Elation sweeps through me when I see the sign for Meyer's. He's taking me to his place.

His house is only a couple blocks away from the shop he owns. Evan opens the door to the nice, two-story house for me and presses his finger to his lips. I see a cane leaning up against the corner beside the front door, and an extra pair of shoes I don't think Evan would wear. His dad lives here?

He leads me upstairs. The house is spacious and gently decorated with soft, blue hues, and Evan has the master bedroom upstairs. Hardwood floor stretches across the space, and the little dresser along the far wall holds a bunch of picture frames. I walk over to them, curious, and pick up a picture of Evan and another guy sitting side-by-side on matching motorcycles. It must be his brother Mickey.

"Dad's got his own place," Evan assures me. "He just sometimes spends the night here. I set him up a spare bedroom downstairs when I moved in, and he stays with me a few nights a month. My house is closer to Meyer's than his is, he reasons, but I think he just gets lonely. I don't mind it."

"That's sweet, Evan." I hold up the picture frame. "Does Mickey live nearby, too?" I don't know much about him at all.

Evan purses his lips and looks down at the floor for a long moment. I stare at him, confused.

Something chills in the air between us. A heaviness weighs the room down as Evan's breath draws harshly, his arms crossed over his chest. Like he's shrinking in on himself, away from me. I've never seen him like this before. Where's my playful, never-hold-back Evan? I tilt my head down, try to catch his gaze.

His shoulders shake. And then I register what this feeling in the air is. It's sorrow. Loss. "Oh, no, Evan, I'm sorry."

He shrugs, but his half a smile doesn't reach his eyes. "You don't know these things unless I tell you, right?"

The way he spoke so warmly of Mickey before when he told me about the habanero pepper eating contest... he was so proud of his family and all its little quirks. Now this cold emptiness presses down on my chest, but it must be nothing compared to what he feels. My heart aches. What happened?

I put down the picture frame and cross the room. I take his hands in mine and wrap them around me, and he sighs deeply into the crook of my neck.

"Do you want to talk about it?"

He shakes his head against my neck. "No, Alice. It's not a story you want floating around your head, believe me."

I hate the darkness in his voice. Possibilities fly through my head. I'm curious to the point of desperation, but I won't push him to open a chapter he isn't ready to share with me yet. Especially not one filled with the pain of losing a brother. I never had siblings, so I don't know that bond firsthand, but I think of Andee. *If she died somehow...* a shiver runs from my ankles all the way up to the top of my head. It's too awful to imagine. "What can I do? Tell me."

He rocks me in his arms. "Just be with me. Just be your stunning, magnetic self, and never push me away."

My heart flips over once at his words. Evan's hands slide across my bare lower back, and then up higher, and he pulls me tight to his body. His lips part, his mouth moving along my neck, and then before I can say anything, I am lost in the intensity of his touch, the way he grabs me like he's terrified he'll lose me if he lets go.

Crash

The weeks rip by in a blur. There is so much to do. The Haven is pretty much a skeleton of a nightclub right now, and it's my job to figure out the interior design and layout of the place. My days are consumed with meetings. Decorators, an architect, interviews with new, prospective employees. That one's the tough part: making sure everyone has a thorough background check done and is totally cool with all aspects of what The Haven is all about. Some candidates walk out as soon as I tell them regular STD testing is part of the job, despite my assurances that there is absolutely *no* sex requirement to be an employee of the club. I find a few security guys right away who are eager to be a part of the place, and good-looking, to boot. Finding matchmakers will be another story altogether. Andee was one-of-a-kind, and I really have to trust a matchmaker before I'm willing to unleash her onto the floor.

Derek doesn't micromanage, but I give him an update every night at The Core. Eventually, he drops my shift back so I only work on the floor until midnight and let Andee handle it until closing, because I'm so busy with preparations for The Haven. I've gotta sleep sometime, so Derek cuts me loose early each night.

Evan comes by most nights when I finish up at The Core. With Andee still working the dance floor until four in the morning or later, we have a few hours to ourselves. He explores me in every way he can, holds me close to him when we finish like I'm the rarest jewel. I cherish every part of his body from his strong, thick arms to the scar on his back. I love running my hands over his back, and he seems to like my touch there, too. He tells me he doesn't fully have feeling on the scar, and it kind of comes and goes. We lie together as the nightlife of the street silences outside, and he hangs onto my every word as I tell him how the preparations for The Haven are going, even when it's really boring shit.

I've never seen anything cuter than when he's pissed off about a snotty customer at Meyer's and starts swearing up a storm.

"I get it," Evan says as he recalls an irritating issue at work, "he wants the fender airbrushed to match the tank. Everybody does, that's fine."

"I didn't realize you did airbrushing, too," I interrupt him.

"Yeah, I started with airbrushing in high school, actually. So this dick monkey has picked out a design, right? For the gas tank. Flaming skulls and chains and shit."

I clap my hand to my mouth to stifle my laughter. Dick monkey?! Where does he come up with these things? "Right."

"And he wants it to match on the fender."

"That's the part that goes over the front wheel?" I'm slowly learning his terminology.

"Or the rear, yeah. Either way, it's a much smaller canvas for me to work on. I can fit a giant flaming skull on the tank, sure, but on this particular fender I can only fit the flames. So I told him that, and you know what the arrogant, shit-eating cock goblin said?"

I can't contain my hysteria, even when he's irritated. I burst into laughter. "What did the shit-eating cock goblin say?" I can barely spit the words out.

"He said, 'Well, maybe I should take the bike to a real artist, then.'"

"God, that's rude. What did you do?"

"I grabbed my prettiest pink ink, loaded it into my airbrush, and asked him if he wanted glitter in the Hello Kitty design for his precious fucking fender."

I roll on top of him, uncontrollably shaking with laughter.

"He grabbed his keys and left. Jackass."

I push up on his chest to peer into his eyes. "You seem even more passionate about motorcycles than cars," I say.

He shrugs and tucks his hands behind his head. "Custom jobs are my favorite. Airbrushing. More people want it done on bikes than trucks or cars."

"Your bike isn't airbrushed," I note.

His expression hardens for a moment, but then he chuckles. "My old one was. I haven't decided what I want on this one, yet."

"I like it plain black, too."

"Do you like it?" He reaches up and tucks a strand of my hair behind my ear. "The bike? Riding with me?"

"I love it." Any time I get a glimpse of the things Evan that turn Evan on, I eat it up like candy.

"Would you want one of your own?"

I've never thought of it. "Maybe someday. I've never ridden, other than on yours."

He grins and slides his hands around my back, stroking my skin. "I have one you can try on, if you'd like. It's smaller, so it will fit you better than mine. It's a classic."

"Is yours not a classic?"

He chuckles. "Mine is a Fat boy."

109

"I'll say."

He laughs again and wraps his hand around the base of my head, kissing me. "Would you like to take another ride on my Fat boy?"

I grin against his lips, tasting his sweet, familiar breath. "Sure. Where are we going?"

He pulls me even closer and lifts my hips to meet his growing erection. "Anywhere you want," he murmurs in my ear, and then he drives himself into me again.

I cry out. He moves in sharp, rhythmic thrusts, clutching me to his chest. I'm so trapped against him his body rubs me in just the right way as he moves. I spiral up to the peak of pleasure fast, and then crash hard around him, clenching him tight with the waves of my orgasm. He groans into my hair, fucks me faster, and finishes with a loud growl, his hands digging into the skin of my hips so tight I never want him to let me go.

"I admire you, Alice," he says to me as we lie on our sides, still glistening with sweat. I'm still having aftershocks. "I don't think I've met many people who could do what you do with such finesse."

My fingers are trapped between his, and he moves them up and down. It's such a tiny touch, our fingers gliding together and then apart, never fully releasing each other. But I watch his hand move and remember those fingers buried inside me, or holding my head still as he kisses me until my lips are deliciously sore. I quake inside, wanting more of him even though I've just had him.

I shrug. "I just dive in and do things. I don't need someone to tell me how... I just figure it out and get it done."

He lets go of my hand and rests his on my side, tracing little patterns with his thumb. "Are you nervous? About opening The Haven?"

110

I think about it for a long time, peering into his eyes. He's so curious about me. Wants to know everything. And the truth is I'm scared as hell. Part of me is convinced I'm going to screw everything up and let everyone who is counting on me down. Derek means so much to me, and he has invested in my future time and time again. If I blow this... fail to make a good impression or screw up the books or have a big, public mishap... *or end up on pills again...* I'll ruin everything he's built. There's so much riding on the success of The Haven I get nauseous just thinking of it.

But hell if I'm going to let Evan see that side of me. The insecure, terrified girl who cops out rather than solving her problems. "Nah. Not really. Opening night will be just like any other night in The Core, except in a new place."

Evan plants a soft kiss on my lips. "This is why I adore you, Alice. You're fucking fearless."

I can't even believe how badly I wish he was right.

Some nights, Evan dozes off beside me and I get to watch the corners of his eyelids crease as he dreams. Some nights, I feel him kiss the corner of my mouth as I'm just falling into the gentle depths of slumber.

He says waking up with me is like starting a new, exciting life every time. I fall deeper in love with him with each passing night, and admire his fearless attitude even more when I see the sunlight spill across his face.

"This is not at all what I meant when I said I'd like to try riding a bike on my own," I say as we stand outside my SUV in the crisp, mountain air one morning. It's Monday, and we've both taken the entire day off to spend it together. I've been working so hard I barely noticed how much time had passed until Evan mentioned it had been over three weeks since we went on an actual date. Lots of fucking, sure, and I've gotten to know him so well in the last few weeks, but it's nice

111

to be outside with him, even if I'm wearing a goddamn bike helmet and looking suspiciously at the path ahead of us. It's a steep climb, but Evan says the hill after it will get my heart pumping so hard it's worth the effort. I haven't been on a bicycle... an actual *bicycle*... in years.

He laughs, tugging playfully on the end of my ponytail. "Well, I've gotta see your balance on an easy bike before I put you on a real bike."

"My balance is fine," I groan.

His eyes tighten a bit at the corners. "I'm not trying to be an ass," he says. "I love mountain biking. It's an even bigger thrill than riding. You'll see."

I peer up at him, skeptical, and he chuckles.

"Come on. I usually camp out here for at least a week in the summer and ride every day. This hill is a total rush. One of my favorites."

"Okay," I relent, my mood brightening. Camping in the wilderness with Evan sounds fun. No chance of waking the neighbors. I rap on the top of my helmet with my fist. "I'm ready as I'll ever be."

Even if I'm not sure about this little adventure, Evan hasn't let me down yet. Everything we do together is exhilarating.

Evan grins at me as he swings his leg over his bike and settles onto the seat. How the fuck can he look so sexy in everything that he does? I vaguely entertain the idea of tossing my bike to the ground and just making love with him in the back of my SUV instead of biking, but I know Evan's been looking forward to this date all weekend. I climb onto my own bike, pedal around in a circle a couple times feeling like a clumsy child, but I get the hang of it quickly. *Huh.* You really do never forget how.

Evan leads the way. Up the mountain path we climb, and I'm surprised my legs aren't burning by halfway up the

112

hill. But dancing at The Core keeps me in pretty awesome shape, and I never have to watch what I eat. Even though I'm running The Haven, I swear I'll never give up the dancing. It's too much a part of my life. My release, like Evan's adrenaline-seeking ways.

We come to the crest of the hill, and the view is breathtaking. We pause at the top to savor it together, parking our bikes and standing side-by-side, and Evan's hand finds mine. I tear my eyes away from the vast, overwhelming valley dotted with a swooping flock of blackbirds and meet his green gaze. He looks severe, and yet happy at the same time.

"Alice," he says.

I stretch up to kiss him, and he seizes my lips eagerly. I take his kiss, push my tongue into his mouth, and delight in the deep groan that escapes him. He captures my chin in his hand as he kisses me, and when we break away, his eyes are ravenous.

"I am going to take you to my house tonight," he says in a tone that warns me there's no arguing with him. My insides heat as he speaks. He grabs me close, his other hand cupping my ass. "I am going to bury myself inside you and fucking stay there all night."

"Good." My voice comes out low, aroused.

"I can't get enough of you. I don't sleep well without you, anymore."

My breath hitches. Does he mean it? Serious moments are so rare with Evan. "Then don't sleep without me anymore."

He searches me as if trying to detect any dishonesty. He kisses me again and then lets me go.

We climb back on our bikes, and I take a deep breath before I start to pedal, willing my focus off my hormones and onto the task at hand. My stomach drops as soon as I look down at the hill before us, but Evan's giddy, encouraging grin is all I need to keep my nerves in check. We're flanked on either side by gentle grass and trees, so even if I bail, I should be able to find a comfortable place to land.

Evan pedals faster, pushing ahead of me and shooting me a daring glance. I try to keep up, and can't restrain an elated laugh as adrenaline spikes through me. The world blurs by as the path grows bumpy, and I try to keep up with Evan. He goes so fast, though, and the hill just goes on and on... my tire catches a rock, and my heart leaps into my throat as I regain my balance.

He moves far ahead of me, whooping with excitement as he tears down the hill. I hit his dust cloud, and sand sticks in my eye, so I bring my hand to my face to swipe it away.

But that's when I hit another rock, my tire bounces hard, and I overcorrect somehow. The bike slides out from under me and skids down the hill, so I let go and yelp as I hit the dirt on my side. Gravity drags me along the bumpy surface of the hill for a moment, and I tumble into a roll. My bike stops before I do, and I crash into it. My foot twists beneath the pedal and something sharp shoots through my ankle. At least the bike stops my descent.

I blink the dust out of my eyes and pain creeps into my awareness. Blood seeps from my thigh where the road has torn through my jeans, and my hands are raw from the ground. But my head seems fine, at least, so I pull myself out from where I'm wedged beneath the bike and start brushing off the dirt. A thick, dull throb starts along the outside of my foot, but I'm able to wiggle my toes.

I'm aware of his heavy footsteps before I see him: Evan racing toward me, his bike discarded at the bottom of the hill.

"Jesus Christ, Alice!" he cries, diving to my side. He grabs my head between his hands, snaps off the helmet, and checks my eyes, panic wrecking his expression.

"I'm okay, I'm fine," I assure him, but he's shaking hard. He grabs me into an embrace and runs his hands down along my arms, panting.

"Your leg," he says. His face is screwed up with disgust, like he's just seen the most terrifying movie of his life.

"It's just a scrape." My voice is tight, choked, and I feel like an idiot that a cry is creeping up my throat after a tumble off a bike. What am I, five?

"I am so sorry, Alice," Evan says, peeling back the edges of my shredded jeans to get a look at the injury. "Son of a bitch, I'm an idiot."

I swallow hard. Shake the emotion away. "It's not your fault. I just lost control, that's all. It's really fine."

Evan scowls at me. "Let's get you home and cleaned up. Did you hit your head? Is your neck okay?"

I force a laugh, but it comes out loaded with humiliation. "Evan, I'm not hurt. No one ever died from a skinned knee. Relax."

His gaze ices, and he stands abruptly. "Let me just grab the bikes. I'll help you up the hill. Don't move." He takes off to go retrieve his bike at the bottom of the hill, and I curse quietly at myself. *Way to ruin a perfectly good day, Alice.*

I get myself standing and gaze up at the hill. I actually made it quite a long way before I wiped out. My bike's pedal is contorted at a funny angle, but everything else seems to be intact, so I start hiking up the hill, pushing my bike along by the handlebars. I wince as the ache sets into my thigh. Worse than that is the thick, swollen feeling in my foot, like I'm walking on a rock. Did I break something? Shit. Evan catches up with me and grabs the bike, carrying both.

It's a quiet drive home. Too quiet. "I'm sorry," I say. "I'll pay to fix the bike."

Evan just glares at me and doesn't say a word. Shit, it's the first time he's ever been mad at me, and I don't know how to deal with it. We haven't had a fight before. Is this a fight? Possibilities spin through my head, and I try not to let my anxiety get the better of me. I decide to just stare out the window, ignore all the little aches and pains emerging in my joints, and wait out his foul mood.

Andee's away at a class when we get home, so I strip off my pants right in the doorway and throw them in the trash. Evan leans on the kitchen counter as I inspect the wound. It's not bad, really, I try to convince myself, even as my foot feels heavier than ever. A ribbon of blood runs down my leg, so I snatch a tissue off the counter and catch the stream, applying pressure. It'll scab like a bitch but then it'll heal over.

"I'm going to take a quick shower," I say. "Wanna join me?" I hook my finger through Evan's belt loop suggestively and try to tug him close, but he doesn't budge. I let go. "Evan, what is it?"

"I should leave," he says.

"Um." I don't know what to say to that. His jaw is set tight with anger. Is this the man who just told me he doesn't sleep well without me anymore? Or did I hit my head and imagine that whole thing? He's never cold to me like this. "Are you mad at me?"

He doesn't meet my gaze. Worry pricks in my heart, and I lean on the counter, too, growing eager to get off my aching foot. "I said I'd fix the bike," I say. "I'm sorry."

He glares at me, and his eyes are furious. I step back. "This has nothing to do with a worthless, piece of shit bike," he snaps.

Whoa. I stammer.

"Alice, I almost got you fucking killed today!"

"Evan, what are you talking about? It's a scrape! A minor injury. I don't even need stitches."

"That doesn't mean anything. It could have been so much worse."

116

"But it wasn't worse. I'm fine."

"And next time, will you be fine? I'm a fucking adrenaline junkie, Alice, and if I drag you into all my dangerous activities, this is just going to happen again."

I can hardly believe what I'm hearing. "What is the big deal, Evan? I know you like adventures. It's half the reason I can't stop thinking about you. I want to see the world through your eyes, enjoy things like you do."

"No, you don't."

"You're not making any sense."

"You don't want to see the things I see! When I saw you rolling down the hill... you don't understand what that's like."

I roll my eyes. Who knew Evan had such a dramatic streak? "So explain it to me."

"No way."

"Why the hell not?"

He lets out a scoff and turns away from me. I gape at him, confused as hell. What is this mood that's swept over him so suddenly? All because I fell off a bicycle? I'm coordinated on the dance floor, but I never pretended to be a master of extreme sports. Why is he making such a big deal out of one little accident?

"You don't want to know this side of me."

"I want to know every side of you." How could I not? Everything about him is intense, enchanting, and intrigues me in ways I never imagined I could be intrigued. Any part of him I can get my hands on, I want.

He lets out a slow, shaky breath, and meets my eyes once more. "You see the side of me I project to you, Alice. You don't want to know the real me. I am a piece of shit. A bad person. The worst kind there is."

"That is *not* true," I say, offended. How can he talk about himself that way? On the other hand, though, I wince at my own hypocrisy. He only sees *this* Alice, too. "Why the hell would you say something like that?"

"Because I got Mickey killed, that's why, and I sure as shit am not going to get you killed, too!"

My mind blanks. Ice slides through my veins, chilling me all the way down to my toes. Oh, fuck. This *is* a big deal. I close the distance between us and try to take his hand, but he jerks it away from me and swallows hard, fighting emotion.

"I'm not just an adrenaline junkie, Alice. There's more to it than that, and you need to know."

I try to lick my lips to speak, but my mouth is dry with fear. Evan refuses to look at me. His shame bears down in the room, and I want so badly to just hold him, if only he'd let me.

"Mickey and I popped a handful of uppers. We were out all goddamn night. And then it was my idea. 'Let's race home,' I said. He was only twenty-two, Alice, your age, and I put him in harm's way so many times."

"I'm sure it wasn't..."

He laughs, a harsh, bitter sound. It leaves a nasty taste in my mouth to hear him like this... the intensity of his joy twisted into something ugly and vengeful. Nausea, cold and unwanted, rushes through my stomach.

"I *knew* I was cutting it close in the intersection," he says. "Thought I'd get through it before the truck got there and Mickey would be stuck waiting for it to pass. But he had a bold streak, you see. And he was so damn competitive. I should have known better... I *did* know better. Mom told me a million times I'd get him killed."

Tears blur my vision, and I don't try to stop them as they fall down my cheeks. *Oh, Evan.* I would wrap him in my arms and weep, if he'd let me.

"So I looked back, and the driver of the truck was slamming on his brakes. I didn't understand that that dark lump rolling across the ground was my little brother. Dead on impact, they said. I see him rolling to a stop every time I fall asleep, over and over. It's on repeat in my brain, and I can't turn it off."

I reach for Evan once more, but again he pulls away, the look on his face one of pure disgust, like he can't stand to have me touch him. "I just stared. He looked so wrong like that, all twisted into a heap. Didn't look where I was going, and I guess that's when I got hit from the other side. All I remember is waking up in the hospital with a tube down my throat. Tubes everywhere. Praying my little brother was in the room next door and in better shape than me."

His lip twists, and tears threaten along the edge of his eyes. "I wrote Mickey's name in the air with my finger. The nurse just said *I'm sorry.* I wrote it again and again. The answer never changed."

I can't hold in my cry. I had no idea, none at all.

Evan scoffs, looking anywhere but at me. "Sorry. Sorry doesn't even come close. I guess I snapped, then, and tried to rip the tube out of my throat, so they had to sedate me deeper. When I got out of the hospital, everything was over... Mickey was already buried, Dad was drowning in sorrow, and I just... I threw myself into work to support him. What else could I do? I killed his son, my own brother. Nothing repairs that kind of hole. Nothing ever will."

The distant glaze over Evan's eyes vanishes as he finally looks at me. "Then I met you. I *sleep* when I'm with you, and I don't see his body tumbling across the pavement anymore. But if I don't leave you now, Alice, I'm gonna be the death of you, too. I can't live with that. I can't have nightmares about both of you."

Panic hits me like a hurricane. He can't be saying what I think he's saying. "That's not going to happen. Nothing bad will happen to me. I'm fine."

"What about the next time I take you out somewhere?" he snaps, angry. "I can't control my need to push things further, harder, faster. If you're caught up in that with me..."

I interrupt, not willing to hear him berate himself further. "I get that this accident reminded you about what happened to him. But it was *not* your fault. I wish I'd been more careful. Just breathe, Evan, and try to look at this when you're calm..." Fear spirals through me. He's slipping away. I want to grab him and never let go.

He holds up his hands and backs away toward the door. "I can't, Alice." His voice cracks.

"Please just wait a minute," I manage, my tears falling in full force, now. "Please don't go. I'll... I'll make coffee, we can talk about this..."

Evan locks his fists at his sides. He's trembling so hard. I push closer to him, grab the leather of his jacket and try to snap him out of it. I take his face in my hands. "Evan, I love you."

His breath is harsh against my face, and I take the opportunity to kiss him. I let my tongue caress his lower lip gently, and I wish I could just pull the pain out of his heart with my kiss. When we part, hope registers in his eyes.

"Do you hear me, Evan? I love you."

His hands slowly unclench, thank God. He lets them slide around my sides and pulls me close. When my lips touch his, his breath finally slows down. He swipes my tears away with his thumbs. I was so scared.

"I couldn't live with myself if anything happened to you," he says between our kisses. Harsh emotion darkens his eyes, and I stroke his smooth, clean-shaven cheeks with my fingertips.

"Nothing will. I was a kid once, you know. Skinned knees every summer."

Finally, he chuckles, and his shaking subsides. Good God, I thought I was losing him. "You were probably one of those fearless kids who drove your mother insane."

I want to make a comment about how I'm sure he was, too, but bringing up his thrill-seeking behavior in light of all I've learned just doesn't seem like the brightest idea I've ever had.

His thumb touches my lower lip. "I made you sad, didn't I?"

"You didn't *make* me anything. I'm so sorry to hear what happened, Evan. It breaks my heart that you're hurting. But I meant what I said."

"You love me." It's a question, even though he doesn't say it that way.

"I do. Everything about you." The truth of it brings a new spark of tears to my eyes, and I will them away.

Evan closes his eyes for a long moment, the space between his brows furrowed, as if he's battling something. He buries his face in the crook of my neck.

"I love you," he says. "How could I *not* love you? You're everything a man could want. But I'm afraid."

I think he's going to say more, but he doesn't so I turn my head and run kisses along his cheek until he can't help but laugh at the tickle of it. "What in the world do you have to be afraid of?"

His hold around me tightens, and I clench inside. There's that intensity I adore.

"What if you realize... in six months, in a year... that I'm not really worth your time at all? You have options, Alice. Guys would kill to be with you. Hell, I would. And they're practically banging down your door."

"Does it bother you?" I wonder aloud. "The male attention I get?"

He shakes his head, pulling back so I can see the sincerity in his expression. "No, that's not what I mean. I know it's part of your job. If I had a job that earned me a lot of female attention, I'd eat it up."

I seize the opportunity for a lighter mood, ignoring the throb in my whole left leg that's starting to demand my attention. "I thought that's what the bike is for. Female attention."

He laughs again. "What I mean is that in six months or a year, *you* might get attention from another guy who catches your eye. Someone more interesting, someone with less baggage."

No more baggage than I have, I think. "I've met plenty of interesting men. None of them do what you do to me, Evan. You aren't going to demand exclusivity from me, I know. But if I offer it to you, will you take it?"

His eyes light with surprise. And then before I can say anything else, he's kissing me madly, his fingers in my hair. "Hell yes, Alice," he breathes, his tongue working its magic along my lips. "Hell yes."

When we come up for air, I'm leaning heavily on him, my foot throbbing harder than before. I try not to think about it.

"Does it bother you?" Evan asks.

"Does what bother me?"

"The male attention. Do the security guys take care of you?"

His intensity has shifted focus now that we're speaking openly about our feelings for one another. *This* is protective-Evan, and I like it. A lot. The way his arms hold me up right now, the concern crinkling the corners of his eyes. It's possessive, hot, and just for me.

"It doesn't bother me. I've never had an incident at The Core where I felt unsafe. But Andee and I have met women who don't appreciate our sexual openness. I'm sure it's mostly born of jealousy, but we've been called sluts a few times."

"And that bothers you."

"Not being called a slut, no." The truth of my own words warms me inside and helps press away the nagging guilt I feel that while Evan is being so open with me, I'm still not telling him anything that matters. "I *love* that men find me attractive. I love that I've had many partners, both male and female. Being called a slut doesn't make me feel any worse than being called dark-haired. It's just a part of who I am: outgoing, sexual, and not afraid of it."

Evan waits for a moment, and then quirks up an eyebrow. "But...?"

"What bothers me is that girls feel the need to insult other girls based on differences. So I've fucked more guys than I can count. I'm not any better than a girl who married her first love. Nor is she better than I am. In The Core, we don't have the right to shame other people for their sexual preferences or fetishes. It doesn't matter. Doesn't define the person or take away from a person's value. But in real life..." I trail off, unsure of where I'm going with this, or what Evan will take from it all.

"In real life, we seem to think it does matter."

"Right." My voice drops to a whisper. "So I worry how you'll feel when you someday introduce me to a friend of yours, and she knows me because I'm that *slut* from The Core."

He nods, understanding. "You think I'll be ashamed of you."

I peer up at him through my lashes, twisting my fingers together nervously.

A grin tugs at the corner of his mouth. "Even though I told Derek I wouldn't come to The Core at all because I was looking for love, not just a one-night-stand."

What? I tilt my head, confused.

He averts his gaze, still smiling, as if remembering something funny. "Even though Derek convinced me I could find love in The Core, from anyone except Alice. Alice isn't into that kind of thing."

"I don't get where you're going with this," I say. My heart pounds with anticipation. I hadn't thought about what Evan was looking for when he decided to show up at my work. I only knew he wanted me when he saw me, and I couldn't resist him even when I tried.

He turns his charming grin on me full-force, taking my breath away. "I *knew* you were untouchable, Alice. But I'm a thrill-seeker. And a challenge like that?" He lets out a satisfied groan, as if re-living a moment of pure ecstasy. "What an unbelievable turn-on."

My mouth falls open. "You came to The Core because Derek... *dared* you? Because he said there was no way you could get me?"

He shrugs, sheepish. "He didn't say it like a dare. I made it into one, I suppose."

A laugh of disbelief escapes me. "And you pulled it off."

"Well, if you still love me after I've told you that... yeah, I think I did."

That's why Derek was so cryptic when I first started dating Evan. I knew there was something going on with him, and I thought maybe it was jealousy, but no... he was just watching himself lose a bet as I fell in love with Evan. I never thought of myself as someone's dare. As an unattainable goal. But the fact that Evan took me on as a challenge to fuel his thrill-seeking needs... it makes me feel like I'm his in more ways than one. A prize. I'm elated, and my heart backflips against my ribs. I lean up and kiss him softly on the lips. "No. The male attention doesn't bother me one bit. Especially not from you."

He takes my mouth with his, holding nothing back, kissing me hard. Yes, I love this man. I want nothing but this man for the rest of my life. I move closer, and my leg fails to hold me up.

Evan catches me. "Let me see that," he says, taking my arms and leading me to the couch. He helps me down, and for the first time since he spoke of Mickey's crash, I realize how badly I'm hurting. It aches all the way through my knee and down to my ankle. My foot is swelling up, and I doubt I'll be able to get it back into my shoe.

He comes back with a warm cloth and an ice pack from the kitchen and kneels between my legs. I hiss with pain when he dabs the cloth against the road rash, and he meets my eyes, lifting my foot and setting it down on top of the ice pack.

"Take it from my experience, Alice... you need to get this checked out."

The thought of hospitals sends a spear of panic through my nerves. I hate the sterile smell of hospitals. I hate needles. I hate the thought of prescription pads and doctors filling out orders for pills. "My leg isn't broken," I protest weakly.

"No, but your foot might be. And it's going to be a pain in the ass to clean all the dirt out of this. Best to get the job done right."

Evan knows road rash better than anyone. I groan and lean back against the couch, throwing my arm over my face. I'm not going to argue with him. Could this suck any harder?

Yes, it could. Evan could have left me. He almost did.

"Well I'm not going to the hospital without pants," I say.

"Are you sure? You'd look adorable on the back of my bike in your panties." He laughs at his own joke.

I take the washcloth off my leg and whip it at him, leaving a wet mark on his shirt. "I'll wear a skirt, thanks." I move to stand up, but he stops me.

125

"I think I know my way to your closet by now." He plants a kiss on the side of my neck and takes off into the bedroom, a skip in his step.

He *does* love me. At least... he loves who I've become.

My Poison

My diagnosis is a bruised femur, a fractured metatarsal in my foot, and my prescription comes in two parts. The first part, I can deal with: antibiotic cream with a steroid to speed the healing of my skin applied three times daily and I have to stay off my feet as much as possible. I don't need a cast, thank God. The second part of my prescription is a little, white piece of paper with a word scrawled in messy, emergency-room doctor handwriting. I don't need to read it to know what it is... painkillers. Narcotics.

I clutch the little piece of paper tight between my fingers as Evan and I wait in line. Maybe if I crumple it enough the pharmacist will refuse to fill it. Maybe I can just say the pain is not so bad. I wince as I wiggle my toes. Even my slippers—that I'm wearing in public, ew—feel too tight.

No such luck, though. The pharmacist verifies my contact information from the computer and makes a copy of my prescription card, and tells me that in ten to fifteen minutes she'll be handing me a bottle of my favorite brand of poison. If Derek didn't provide me with such fantastic employee benefits, I could have gotten away with saying I couldn't afford the pain pills. But nope. My boss is just that fantastic.

I re-fill my birth control pills while I'm at it, and Evan winks at me with approval.

Evan and I browse the pharmacy while we wait. I'm limping, so he holds my hand, and I try my best to hide my anxiety.

"I'm sure Andee can handle The Core on her own for a few days," he says. "Derek will understand."

I blink at him, surprised. He doesn't know what's really bothering me though, so I cover it with a chuckle. "Yeah, I'm sure he will. I just..." *Come on, Alice...* "I just hate missing out. Dancing is such a big part of my life."

"Well, you have six to eight weeks to fill that part of your life with something else." He hooks his finger into the strap of my tank top and tugs me close, narrowing his eyes with salacious desire. "However will we kill that much time?"

"You still have to work."

"During the days. I get you all night long with no competition from The Core?" He does a triumphant fist pull, and for a moment, I can almost see life the way he does. Six to eight weeks of just us in the evenings, uninterrupted by the sexual needs of others... it's like we've won the lottery. But it's not that simple. If I take these pills, I'll drift off into oblivion. Who says I'll be able to stop at all?

I sigh. "I'm no good to The Core or The Haven if I'm loopy on pain meds." It's half a truth, but oddly, I feel a little bit better now that I've said it.

He snorts. "Loopy Alice sounds more entertaining than a Saturday matinee. Besides, it's only a few days of the meds. Ibuprofen will take the edge off once the healing starts."

I shake my head, desperate to change the topic. I want to ask him about his own road rash and the healing process, but that would remind him of Mickey. I almost lost him to the grief just hours ago. I pluck a box of cherry-flavored condoms off the shelf. Evan snorts and takes it from me, tucking it back where it belongs.

"I like my manhood Alice-flavored, thanks."

128

I burst into laughter, startling everyone in the Family Planning aisle of the pharmacy.

Evan drops me off at home. My purse is heavier than usual. Like, five thousand times heavier. How can a few days' worth of pills weigh so much?

"You sure you won't let me stay with you tonight?" Evan asks, his green eyes sparkling with concern.

I want so badly to ask him to stay. "I'm sorry," I say. "I really need to sleep. I'd just tap out on you early anyway."

He nods, but I can tell he's not happy about my decision. I give him a slow kiss, pouring as much apology through it as I can. "I'll text you in the morning," I say.

Evan slips his helmet back onto his head. "Okay. Have fun."

"I will." Not too much fun, I hope.

I wave at him as he peels away. Inside, Andee's just pulling a casserole dish out of the oven. The scent of baked pasta hits me and my mouth waters right away. I haven't eaten since early this morning before my epic fail of a bike ride.

"Hey!" She stops when she sees me and stares, taking in the sight of my dirty tank top. I neglected to change it before we went to the hospital. "Whoa, what happened to you?"

I limp toward the bedroom. "I was riding a bicycle," I say.

Andee chuckles. "You're calling Evan a bicycle now? That's not very nice."

"Ha-ha," I say. "Really. I fell in the mountains. Gotta stay off my feet for a few days."

"Oh, shit, Alice," Andee says. "Are you okay?"

I wave her off. "Yeah, just some antibiotic cream and I'll be fixed right up." My toes go cold as I omit a critical part of the truth from my best friend. "You don't mind if I just hit the sack, do you? I'm fucking exhausted."

Andee peels the tinfoil lid off the pasta, steam billowing out. "No, of course not. Get some rest. Are you hungry? Do you need anything?"

"Nah, just my pillow. Thanks, Andee." My stomach rolls. Hungry as I was a moment ago, lying to Andee is too much for my appetite to handle.

I close my bedroom door and set my purse on the mattress. Get myself a glass of water from the bathroom. Sit down. Open the bag, pull out the bottle. Read the label twenty times.

Am I really going to do this?

These pills were prescribed to me, I reason. By a doctor, for a real injury. I didn't fake a migraine to get them, nor did I buy them off the street. The bottle actually says my name, not the name of a widow who left a pile of prescription drugs behind for her adult children to sell. I did nothing wrong today.

Nothing wrong yet. If I swallow one of these little, white pills, I'll be letting myself slide down into a rabbit hole that doesn't have a way out. I should lock these pills in my bottom drawer at The Core and throw the key off a mountain.

My leg throbs with urgency as if to sway my decision. I put the bottle on my nightstand, shuffle out of my skirt, and apply some of the cream to my wound. Curling up on my side, I stare at the little orange bottle and read my name over and over again.

I can't sleep with these pills in the room. I could sleep if Evan was here, but he'd insist I take one of them. I wouldn't be able to argue with him without letting something slip out. I'm damned if I do, and I'm damned if I don't.

My foot really does hurt.

So I flip the lid off the bottle, put just one pill on my tongue, and swallow it down. It tastes like failure, but as the medicine warms my blood, my bed starts to feel softer than it ever has before. My pain subsides. All the worrying was for nothing. I'm not behaving like an addict. I'm being a good patient, following my doctor's orders. I have nothing to be ashamed of.

I wake two hours later, the throb in my leg returning with a vengeance. I try to find a comfortable position. Every way I turn pulls the skin on my thigh tight, and makes my foot ache anew. The medication bottle says I should only take one pill every four to six hours. But I was sleeping so peacefully, and I need sleep if I'm going to heal. I know I have kind of a high tolerance for narcotics, anyway. That light, airy feeling of nothing holding me down would help me drift back into a deep, soothing slumber.

So I take another one.

The bottle of pills is empty by morning.

I wake with my head pounding a solid beat, like a fist on wood. *No, wait, that's the door.* Someone's knocking on the door. Why hasn't Andee answered it?

I tumble out of bed onto my knees. Pain shoots through my leg, but I ignore it and reach up to find my alarm clock. It says five o'clock, but I could have sworn I took my last few pills at ten. What the hell is going on?

Pounding again. "Alice!" Derek's voice booms through the apartment. Oh, shit! The sunlight outside my window is fading to orange... it's five o'clock in the evening, and I've wasted the day away in a fog of prescription drugs.

"Just a second!" I call. I scramble for a pair of jeans and yank them on, forgetting my injured leg. The denim scrapes along my wound and I yelp, dropping back to the floor. I kick off the jeans, grab some sweatpants out of the dirty laundry pile, and stagger to the door.

Derek stands with his hands pressed to either side of the door frame, seething with anger. I back inside the apartment and gesture for him to come in, trying to straighten my hair into something presentable.

Derek slams the door behind him.

"So," he says, his hands planted on his hips, "Evan came into The Core this afternoon, looking for Andee."

"Did he?" My voice sounds too high-pitched. Guilty.

"He was freaked out that he hasn't heard from you since yesterday, but didn't want to just show up unannounced."

Shit. "My phone must be dead. I'll text him right away. Sorry, Derek, thanks for letting me know." Am I slurring my words? No, I'm being paranoid. I'm fine.

He glares at me, and my heart pounds so hard I'm afraid I'm going to crack a rib. "Yeah, Andee said you were still sleeping when she left this afternoon," he says.

"It was a really long day yesterday." Everything sounds like a lame excuse when it comes out of the mouth of an addict.

"Anything else you want to tell me about?"

I shake my head.

My boss scowls at me. "Nothing about a little trip to the pharmacy with Evan? I thanked him for taking such good care of you."

Son. Of. A. Bitch. I am busted.

"Give me the pills, Alice."

"I didn't take them," I insist.

Fury flares in his eyes. "Don't lie to me. You never miss work. You're high as a fucking kite. Give me the pills."

"I'm not high!" Lying to Derek tastes even worse than lying to Andee. "I'm injured. I'm sorry, I should have called you."

Derek slams a fist down on the counter beside the kitchen. I jump.

"Alice, for God's sake, I *know* you. I did not invest years of my time and energy into your sobriety for you to blow it now. Give me the motherfucking pills, or so help me I'll turn this apartment upside down until I find them."

My careful defensiveness morphs into anger so quickly I don't have time to think before I speak. "As if you *minded* getting me sober, Derek. You fucked me for a solid week to help me straighten out. That doesn't give you some kind of authority over what I should or should not do in my spare time."

His anger burns even hotter in his dark eyes. "You *asked* me to distract you from the withdrawals. That's exactly what I did. I don't have any authority over you? Where the fuck would you be without me? In the gutter? Dead? You owe me the truth, at least."

"I don't owe you anything!" I scream it at him, furious. "I don't need *shit* from you!"

The rage in his eyes ices over, and he chuffs with disbelief. "I knew this was a bad idea to begin with. Putting all my stock into a junkie. I told myself you weren't like that... you were a good girl who got caught up in some bad shit. Clearly, I was wrong."

My own words echo back into my ears. Was that really me, screaming like an ungrateful bitch at my boss—my friend—who has given me the benefit of the doubt time and time again?

"Did you want to start this conversation over, Alice? Or should I re-evaluate my investments in the future of my business?"

The blood drains from my face, and I steady myself against the counter. How could I talk to Derek that way? I got defensive and yelled at him to mask my own failure. Derek has done far more for me than I have earned. I duck my head, staring at patterns in the carpet.

"Give me the pills," Derek repeats, his voice gentler.

A cry of humiliation works its way up my throat, choking me. "I can't," I whisper.

His hand catches mine. "Yes, you can." I wish, with all my heart, that I could be soothed by his tone, his unconditional understanding of my constant fucking-up. "I know you can. You're stronger than this addiction."

The carpet spins in my vision. I sink to my knees, burying my face in my hands. I try to rub some feeling back into my cheeks. Everything's numb. Shame, cold and nauseating, skewers me from the inside out. "No, Derek, I can't. I don't have them."

The apartment is quiet for a moment as he processes this. When he speaks again, he's right beside me on the floor, his arm solid and strong around my shoulders. "You took them all?"

I can't lie to him anymore. He sounds far away as the painkiller still fogs my awareness.

"All of them."

"Goddammit," Derek says, but he sounds frightened than angry. "How many? I'll take you in."

"No, not that many," I say. Weight lifts off my lungs as I open up to him, but the last thing I want is my stomach pumped. Or the Spanish Inquisition from the hospital staff. "It was a few days' worth. I took them slowly."

He doesn't say anything for a long moment. I start to doze against his shoulder, so he shakes me awake. I struggle to open my eyes.

"Wake up. It's time to go."

"I don't want to go."

"Sorry, Alice," Derek says, "but you don't have a choice in this, today."

I don't remember getting into his truck or checking into the hospital. The next thing I know, I've got an IV in a vein and my mouth tastes like charcoal. It was too late to pump my stomach, but the little black capsules keep the remaining medication from doing much damage, they tell me. Derek sits

134

in a chair beside my hospital bed, gently stroking my hair. I refuse the hospital's offer for inpatient treatment. I've been sober for so long... I can do this on my own. I know I can. Pain surges in my foot, angry and demanding, as if to discourage me.

"Please don't tell them," I beg Derek when we're alone. "Please."

He shakes his head. "You should tell Andee and Evan."

"Andee knows about my issues," I say. "But I don't want her to think of me like this. I was such a bitch, Derek. I'm sorry."

"You know I don't hold it against you." He sighs. "The drugs do their own share of talking when you're high. But even though you're my friend, Alice, try to put yourself in my shoes. Think of the trust I'm placing in you with The Haven."

"I know. And I know I don't deserve another chance. But I swear to you, Derek, this will be the last time you're disappointed in me. I swear."

He purses his lips, considering. "You should take them up on the offer for treatment. I'll pay for it if our benefits won't cover it. Every dime."

"And if I don't?" I meet his brown eyes. Is he taking The Haven away from me? Though I know he can afford it, I don't want to go to treatment. How the hell would I keep up with work and Andee and Evan if I was locked up discussing my mommy issues with some white-suited therapist?

It takes Derek a minute to form an answer, and when he does, he gives me a look of sincerity I know way better than to question. "This is your last strike, Alice. Next time you fall off the wagon, I will not scrape your ass off the floor. I trust you can still do your job. But I will not sit here with you again, and I will not hand the keys to my multi-million-dollar establishment over to a junkie. If I find you high even once after this, we're done."

The finality in his tone sinks into me like ice, but relief pushes my fear away. I still have my job. I still have my friend. I reach out and find his hand, and he strokes my knuckles with his thumb, careful of the IV. I thank him over and over again.

Old Wounds

It takes me a couple days to be ready to face the world. Deep down, I know this is withdrawal... my old dependence on the drugs surging forth with a vengeance. But I try to reason that I had an injury, and that I had two visits to the hospital, and it's really okay if I take it slow. The hardest part is falling asleep... and staying asleep. But Evan was right: after two days, ibuprofen is all I need to take the edge off the pain.

I pull up to Meyer's garage and park a half a block away. I've exchanged text messages with Evan, but I haven't seen him. He seems suspicious of me, and probably feels like I have started to pull away from him. Which I guess is kind of true, but not for the reasons he fears. I park the Escalade and lock the doors. Derek really had a point: where would I be without him? Not pulling up to my boyfriend's work in a beautiful SUV dressed in designer jeans and a tight, white blouse looking like a million bucks, that much is certain. Derek has paid me well for the work I've done. With all the chances he's given me, and I owe it to him to do my absolute best in everything.

I've never been to Meyer's before. Lots of banging and whirring sounds come from the two open bays, and I see legs in dark blue coveralls sticking out from beneath a couple vehicles. I thought I'd know Evan when I walked up, but seeing just the legs has me uneasy. Which one is he? I make my way through the doors of the little lobby—still limping a bit—and sit down. It's a nice shop with a coffee machine and a little bowl of candies on the desk. An elderly man pushes through the door from the garage to the lobby, stops when he sees me, and breaks into a big, toothy grin. He wears little glasses and has short-cropped, white hair, and sure enough, he looks just like Evan.

"Well, hello, Miss." He closes the door behind himself, shamelessly checking me out.

I can't help but giggle. I stand and hold out my hand to shake his. "I'm Alice," I say. "Here to see Evan."

He takes my hand and brings it up to his knuckles, giving me a quick kiss. "Eddie Meyer," he says. "Evan's busy. But I'm free as can be."

Eddie must be Evan's dad. He's adorable. Like a little, old Evan. I turn the awkward hand embrace into a firm shake and then let go. He puts on a pout as I pull my hand away.

"I can come back later, if you'd prefer," I say, giving him a genuine smile.

"Or you're welcome to keep me company while you wait for him?" He flashes that charming grin again—it must be a genetic trait—with an eyebrow cocked upward.

Evan pushes into the lobby. "Okay, old man, no scaring off my girlfriend."

I stride to his side and wrap my arms around his middle, enjoying the feel of his body against me. I've missed him. He doesn't hug me back, but he's holding a dirty rag and his hands are coated in black grease so I can't blame him.

"Not scarin' her off!" Eddie protests. "We were just getting to know one another." He winks at me, and I return it.

"Don't mind Dad," Evan murmurs to me. "He was a dirty old man before he was old."

"I heard that," Eddie barks, feigning hurt. "Breakin' my heart, kid."

Evan laughs and leads me outside. I give Eddie a wave over my shoulder, and he blows me a big, dramatic kiss.

"He's harmless," Evan explains. "He just also thinks he's lovable enough to get away with anything."

"He is awfully cute."

He chuckles. "Hope you still think so when I'm old and grouchy."

"Nah, you won't be grouchy. You'll be a dirty old perv like your dad." I elbow him playfully.

Evan's smile falls. "Where have you been, Alice? I've been worried about you."

Shit, here we go. "I'm sorry," I rush. "Please don't be angry with me."

"How could I be angry with you? You're the one who has the right to be angry with me. I told you some shit you probably never wanted to know about me, and then you pulled away. I can't say I blame you, but..."

Oh, no. He thinks I feel less for him now that I know about Mickey. I've been so wrapped up in my own bullshit that I've been neglecting Evan after he opened up to me. "That's not it. I know it looks bad, but honestly, Evan, I just needed some time."

"Why?" He finishes wiping his hands and stuffs the rag into the pocket of his coveralls. "Don't tell me you think we need time apart. I've had enough of that shit this week to last me a lifetime."

Always so direct. His words warm my heart, but at the same time, send a twisting pang of sickness through my stomach that I'm still lying to him. It's do or die time... I have to either tell him the truth now... all of it... or bury it and never let it out. If I let this go on any longer, he won't be able to forgive me when it finally comes out.

"No, we don't need time apart. At least, I don't think so. But I do need to talk with you about a few things. Can you come over tonight? I'm working at The Core for the evening shift but I'll be done before midnight."

A frown creases his forehead, darkening his beautiful, green eyes. "This doesn't sound good. I'm dying with anticipation over here. Just tell me."

I glance back at Evan's dad, still watching us warily through the window. Flirtatious as he may be, I see the protectiveness in his eyes as Evan's anxiety visibly increases.

"Not here," I say. "And don't worry. It's really not about you. We're fine." *For now.*

"Some other guy?"

My heart just about stops. "Why the hell would you jump to that conclusion?" His words about male attention come back to me, and I have to swallow hard to press the surge of indignity away. "I wouldn't cheat on you, Evan. You know that."

He holds up his hands in surrender, frustrated. "I'm sorry. I end up at worst-case scenario irrationally sometimes. I know you wouldn't. I just... I guess I've been wondering the last few days if we're still together at all."

God, I'm an asshole. I deserve his sharp words. I step closer to him, stretch up, and welcome a long, chaste kiss from his lips. "Yes, of course we're still together. I just need to get some things off my chest, that's all. I love you."

He closes his eyes, and for a moment, he almost looks like he's in pain. When he opens them, his gaze is hot, hungry—and just the way I love it—only for me.

"I'd slam you up against the wall right now and kiss you until you couldn't breathe, if I wouldn't get you all dirty doing it."

Heat floods my cheeks. I've missed his confidence, the last few days. I forget all about his accusation. "I like to get dirty."

He chuckles and kisses me again. I'm both relieved and disappointed when he doesn't make good on his threat, greasy hands and all. "Okay, I'll pick you up at The Core tonight. Sound good?"

I can't help the excitement bubbling up through my mood. But even though he's coming over, I don't know that he'll stick around after I tell him all the bullshit I wish I could hide. He needs to know. I kiss him again in reply, wave affectionately at Evan's dad, who looks sterner now, and take off to my SUV.

All I can do is hope Evan forgives me for lying to him, and understands why I did it. I pull out into the street and head for The Core. At least there, I'm free of the drama, and free of the bullshit. I need to clean out my office tonight and open a new chapter for myself in all ways.

The Core is pulsing with life when I get inside. Opening time. I am greeted by several regular patrons and all the staff members, and welcomed back with a huge hug from Andee. I should probably come clean with her too, I think, but now is not the time, and here is not the place. I give Derek a big, enthusiastic wave across the bar, and his nod of greeting is warm and approving. I'm still too sore to hit the dance floor, but I can have a good time on my last night here even if it's a little bit slower.

The Core doesn't pick up to a manic pace, tonight... it's a quieter group of people, and though we keep the dancing going and the alcohol flowing, it stays pretty calm. I get a few breaks to sit and rest my foot, so it doesn't bug me too much. By midnight, most of the patrons are paired up and leaving together, with just a few regulars hanging around. So many of the customers in our vibrant, bright atmosphere come because they know there are other people out there who haven't opened up yet, who need to cut loose. Even Christopher doesn't mind if he doesn't get laid when he's here, as long as he's available for anyone who needs him. It's such a loving environment, in its own way. I lean on the railing overlooking the dance floor from above, and watch Andee walk a couple to the door. The brilliant colors of the graffiti walls contrast with the black leather and chrome décor.

I've had such a colorful time here. I can't wait to open The Haven and start a new chapter. I have so much to do... it's why Derek offered me this as my last shift, but is keeping up my wage as I start on the daytime work of prepping the new club. It's still got a long way to go, but I have opening night scheduled for three months from now.

I peer down at the entry hall, and through the curtains steps the most flawless, panty-droppingly beautiful man in the world. Evan. I wave to him with a bit more excitement than I intend, and spring into step, taking the stairs down two at a time. Derek beats me to his side, and my grin melts as I take in the anger on my boss's face.

"What the hell are you doing here?" Derek demands.

Evan looks between me and him, but I'm just as confused. "I'm here to pick up Alice. What's it to you?"

I glare at Derek. I'd like to know the answer to that, too.

"You need to leave," Derek says. "You've done quite enough for her. I don't want to see you back here again."

Evan's eyes go wide with fury, and he takes a step closer to me, but Derek gets in his way, stopping him with a hand to the chest.

"Back off, man," Evan snaps, batting Derek's hand away.

"Derek, wait," I try to interject, but my boss is furious. Andee swoops in to stand at my side, and we've caught the attention of a few of the security staff.

142

Derek glares at Evan. "Get the fuck out of my club. You expect me to let you anywhere *near* Alice?"

"Derek, stop!" It's like no one hears me.

Evan holds up his hands with innocence. "I don't know what you're talking about, but you better get the hell out of my way, Derek. We've been friends for a long time. You told me you were cool with the two of us, so back off."

"I changed my mind."

"Well, un-change it. She's mine."

Does Derek not understand that already? I am Evan's. Entirely.

"I was cool with the two of you before you almost got her killed. You pack her fucking purse with *drugs* and then have the nerve to show up here? I'm not letting her anywhere near you."

Whoa! Shit! Derek blames Evan for me getting high. "That's *not* what happened!" I shout.

Derek ignores me. He plants both his palms in Evan's chest and shoves him back, hard.

Evan's eyes flare with anger as he recovers from the shove, and it all happens so fast. Evan slams a fist into Derek's face, and Derek gets a swing in before security tackles Evan to the floor. Andee yanks me back, but I scream, batting her off. I climb into the pile of shouting, wrestling men and shove the security guys away. Evan recovers, wiping blood from his mouth with the back of his hand.

"I'm fine," he snaps, glaring at me.

I jump up and turn on Derek. "What the hell is this?" I demand. "Who the fuck put you in charge of my love life, Derek? Evan did *nothing* to hurt me. The other day, the pills... that was all me, not him. He doesn't even know, and it wasn't your fucking business to tell him!"

"Tell me what?" Evan's voice is furious, and he rises to his feet. Andee gapes at me.

Fuck.

"Go ahead, Alice," Derek says. "I warned you: I will *not* scrape your ass off the ground again. You're the one who's supposed to be accountable for this shit, and he can't be in your life if he doesn't know what he's dealing with. If you won't tell him, I have to, or the two of you are through."

I want to scream at him for being so fucking controlling. This isn't his problem. Not his business.

But I made it his business when I promised him my sobriety. I made it his problem. And he's right: in order to protect myself from this happening all over again, I have to be accountable. I have to be honest. I scowl at him, but then I turn to face Evan. I put my hand on his arm, and he practically vibrates with restrained rage.

"Can we talk? Please. Let's go somewhere private."

He jerks his arm away from me. "We can do this right here, Alice. Why the fuck is this assdonkey accusing me of *drugging* you? I would never do something like that. What the hell have you been telling people about me?"

I glance around. The security guys back off, seeing that the situation has settled and I need some privacy. Derek leans against the bar, watching, his eyes stern, and Andee puts her hand on the small of my back.

"Do you want me to go?" she asks.

What would I do without Andee? She's the only one in the goddamn room giving me even a shred of dignity. "No, don't go," I say. "You need to hear this."

Evan huffs, still furious. I swallow hard and take a deep breath.

"I'm an addict, Evan. Pain pills. I've been sober for a couple years, but when Derek met me, I was... rock bottom. I hated the person I was. You would have hated me." My voice sounds far away, like it's not really mine.

Disappointment—or revulsion, I can't tell which—twists his expression into something shocked.

No going back now. My pulse beats so hard the room jumps. "I was terrified to tell you, so I didn't say anything when we picked up my prescription."

"And you just let Assdonkey over there think I was providing you with drugs."

Andee giggles at the nickname, but then whispers an apology. I wish I could laugh with her, break the tension. But this is too important, and as much as I want to reach out, grab Evan's hand and drag him back into my changing room for a reassuring fuck, I can feel him pulling away. My heart throbs.

"No, that's on him. But Derek did come find me the day after I fell."

Alarm registers on Evan's face. "What the hell did you do?"

My mouth goes dry, but Andee nudges me with her shoulder, encouraging me to be strong. "I took all the pills. Ended up in the emergency room."

He flinches like I've smacked him. "You did *what?*"

"I'm an addict, Evan, I can't be around them, and I know I should have told you..."

"You think?" He scoffs. "After everything I told you about my own bullshit... you held out on me and put yourself in a life-threatening situation just to hide this from me?"

I don't even have an excuse. "I'm sorry..."

"Fuck sorry!" Evan shouts at me, furious. "Alice, you *lied* to me. I told you about Mickey... why didn't you say something then? You let me yap on and on about how the pain pills would help... you could have died."

"I know. But I didn't. And I won't. I'm sober as can be, and I'm not going to fall back on those patterns again. Evan, I love you. Please let me have another chance... I won't let you down. Any of you."

I hear Derek blow out a slow breath, and Andee's hand rubs my back supportively.

Evan's eyes shift between mine for a moment, and then he steps closer. I reach for him, but when I touch his chest, he's hard. Unresponsive to my caress. I pull my hand back. It's like he's burned me.

"Alice," he whispers, his penetrating glare ice cold, "you had the audacity to be angry with me today for questioning the trust we have built between us. And then you tell me you *lied* to me all along. Where the hell does that leave me?"

"I don't know," I say, my voice rough like I've been screaming. "Where does it leave you?"

He looks between Derek and me again, and then lets out a frustrated sigh. "Alone."

"Evan, wait." I start after him as he turns his back on me, but he moves too quickly. He doesn't want to be followed. Andee's hand rests on my shoulder, and I let her pull me back.

"Alice," Derek says.

"Fuck you," I spit at him.

"It needed to be done. You had to tell him."

"I *know* that," I snap. "But I had the right to do it in my own time, in my own way, and without anyone getting black eyes over me." Derek's eyelid is already puffing up, and it gives me a little, bitter surge of pride that Evan clocked him a good one for overstepping himself the way he did. "I was going to tell him tonight. You had no right to bombard him like that."

"And Andee? When were you going to tell her?"

I peer at Andee, and my face flushes hot with humiliation. My best friend, my roommate... I should have told her when it happened. Hell, I should have handed her the pills when I walked in the door that day and let her protect me. She wouldn't have blamed me for needing help.

"Honestly, Derek?" Andee says. "If Alice didn't tell me something, I trust that she had a damn good reason for withholding it. Maybe she just needed more time. Either way, I don't have the right to humiliate her in front of her boyfriend like that, and neither do you." She slaps down the glass in her hand on the bar and stomps past him.

Derek finally averts his eyes from me. I take the moment to push beyond him and get away from his accusatory attitude. I hope no one outside our circle of staff saw this little altercation, but I have my doubts. A few patrons still linger in the booths.

I shut myself in my office. The emptiness sucks me in. How could all this have happened so quickly? I thought I had such control over my actions, my surroundings, and my addiction. But all it took was one accident... one little, tempting bottle of pills... and everything is screwed up.

I have to get out of here. I pack up my office. Who knows if Derek is still handing The Haven over to me after this? The only thing I can do is carry on as though he is, and hope my confidence in myself is enough to convince him. I toss everything I own in a box and pull out the suitcase I keep in the closet, loading it full of my spare changes of clothes, my makeup, my things in the bathroom. And then I thumb the little key dangling off my wrist, and stare at the bottom drawer of my desk.

I haven't opened it. Not since I filled it up. How fucking stupid I've been. But I can't just leave all this there for Andee or Derek to deal with, so I blow out a harsh breath, kneel down, and stick the key in the lock.

The Ziploc bag looks the same as I left it... sealed with a bunch of orange, almost-empty prescription bottles inside. I run my thumb over the plastic, reading a label. Everything's long expired, but that never stopped me before. It's like finding an old diary. I want to crack each one open and explore the person I used to be.

I can't do that, though. I have to get rid of them. I shove the bag into my purse, zip it closed. I won't look at them again. I'll take them straight home and flush them down the toilet, like I should have done years ago. I drop my purse on top of the box, drag all my shit out into the hallway, and savor one last affectionate gaze around the office. Andee's office, now.

I push through the curtain at the end of the office hallway, and jump when Andee greets me there, a shot glass in her hand.

"You look like you need to drown your sorrows a little bit," she says over the music.

I eye the shot glass suspiciously. "You're not mad at me?"

Andee shrugs. She's so easy-going. "I'm not happy you didn't trust me with this when it happened, but I know you. I know you probably didn't tell me because you thought it would change our friendship somehow."

So perceptive, as always. "Oh, Andee, what the hell am I going to do? I've fucked everything up."

She passes me the shot glass, so I clink the edge of it with hers and down the liquid. It's sweet and delicious, and reminds me of the taste of Evan's lips.

"You're going to get shitfaced with your best friend and forget all this boy bullshit. Derek went home to lick his wounds, and everyone else is gone but security. So down the hatch it goes."

Her attitude is so infectious. I return her grin and peer at the empty shot glass. "What was that?" I shout over the music.

"A Cowboy Cocksucker," she explains. "Butterscotch, vanilla vodka, and Irish cream. You want another?"

148

Nothing about this night has gone well, but the alcohol warms me inside. I don't need any more persuasion than that. I slam the shot glass down on a nearby table. "Hell yeah, I do!"

The drinks go down like dessert, they're so good. I dance carefully with Andee. I let her energy sweep me away. The Core is so vibrant when we're both spinning with carefree joy. I cherish every whirl of the disco ball, every flash of the strobe lights, and every time I crash drunkenly into the neon graffiti-painted walls. By the time the sun is peeking over the horizon, I can barely see the path ahead of me, but my foot doesn't even hurt anymore, and neither does my heart.

I am so unbelievably drunk. It strikes me as hilarious that I have a suitcase packed to leave work, and I entertain myself for a few minutes bidding The Core farewell, telling the big, bright nightclub that it never could have worked out between us anyways. I vaguely notice I have a bottle of vodka in my hand, so I tuck it back behind the bar somewhere and grab my purse.

Andee helps me stumble to a cab on the curb, and I throw myself into her arms. She must be far soberer than I am. More sober? *Whatever.* She pulls away and buckles me into the cab. "Go home and drink a shitload of water. I'll be there soon."

I roll down the window and high five her before the cab pulls away. I find my phone in my purse and flip through the texts. My finger lands on Evan's name, so I open it up and read through them. He hasn't texted me, and the longer I stare at his sweet words of anticipation for the next time he was supposed to see me before the fight with Derek, the more irritated I grow.

Not just irritated. I get mad. *Drunk* mad. He thinks he's the only one with problems. He thinks he's the worst person on the planet for an accident that, frankly, was as much Mickey's fault as his. Well, I'm that person too: a pill-popping junkie failure, just trying to scrape by. Trying to repair holes that can

149

never be filled, just like him. He has no right to judge me for my dishonesty, and I decide I have to tell him that, *right now.* Straighten him out so at least he knows who's really a bad person, here. I try to text him, but the damn screen keeps putting the wrong letters in the words, so I smack it a couple times. That doesn't improve my texting skills. I scowl.

Mickey's death was a tragic accident. Everything I've ever done, I did with intent. Evan is not the wicked witch in this relationship. I am. But to walk off on me for wanting to hide that fact... for wishing he could see me—at least for a little while—as better than my dark past just isn't fair. Would he have told me about Mickey if I hadn't crashed that damn bike? No! We'd be *fine* if he wasn't so prone to overreacting.

In the back of my mind, I recognize this is a bad idea, but I'm too angry to care. I tap the driver of the cab on the shoulder and give him Evan's address. When we pull up to the curb, I leave my purse in the car and tell the driver to just wait a minute, I won't be long.

Evan answers the door wearing nothing but flannel pajama pants. I giggle when I see him: he's so gorgeous. "You know, I wanted to fuck you into oblivion tonight." It feels like it's been so long without him.

Evan glances back at the cab driver, and then narrows his eyes at me. "Are you high?"

Even though I expected it, his words hit me like a slap. "Fuck you. I'm drunk, and I'm allowed to be. This is exactly why I didn't want to tell you."

"Sorry. I didn't mean... wait, *should* you be drunk after what happened?"

I scoff and give him a dramatic shrug, ignoring the way the concern in his voice lures me in. "You know, there are *so many* worse things I could be right now. And I don't really think you're one to judge."

He sighs. "Alice, come on. I'll follow the cab on my bike and make sure you get home."

"I don't need your fucking *rescuing*, Evan. I am doing just fine on my own, thanks."

"Looks like it," he says, taking in my appearance. I glance down. My shirt is stained with some kind of booze that makes up a Cowboy Cocksucker and I'm not wearing any shoes. I wonder where they are. Hm...

The cuteness of his half-naked self wears off as suddenly as it came on. "Evan, you seem to think..." I jab a finger into his bare pec, "...that you're the only one who's fucked up. I get that you think I'm a bitch for lying to you."

Evan sighs. "Try to see this from my point of view. I've lost too much already. And I am so unbelievably in love with you... if I lost you, what the hell would I have left?"

"So you're just throwing me away."

He glares at me, and I think I see anger flashing in his eyes. *Good.*

"I *have* to. I almost got you killed twice... once on that stupid bike, and again when I practically handed you a bottle of poison to drink."

"I took that poison myself! That was me, nothing to do with you, and you cannot take the responsibility of that away from me! How the fuck am I ever going to kick this for good if I let people blame it on *anything* other than that I have a goddamn problem?"

Evan pales, but I'm too far gone. The dam's broken. There's no stopping it now.

"You think I don't understand what it's like to hate yourself for a past you can't do anything to change?"

He stammers, but I don't give him a chance to put the brakes on. My voice escalates as the shame—buried so deep for years—vomits out.

"I'm such a goddamn addict I used to suck dick for pills."

Evan stares at me, wordless.

"You heard me. Suck. Dick. For. Pills."

"Alice, you don't have to..."

"No, Evan, you want my honesty, that's exactly what you're gonna get. I lived on the street and screwed more dealers than your pretty little imagination can dream up. My own mother ran *screaming* away rather than watch her whore of a daughter kill herself slowly with pain pills. Or hell, maybe she just didn't want to identify my body when I ran out of cash to pay for what I took. Maybe she didn't want me sending her the fucking dental bill if I got my teeth stomped out. I guess I can't blame you for doing the same!"

Evan sucks in a breath of surprise at my rant. He straightens and reaches for my hand. But like he did to me, I jerk away. *Ha! How does it feel?*

The hurt registers on his face, and I regret it immediately. I didn't come here to cause him more pain. "Evan, I love you," I say, my voice failing. "I've fallen in love with you, and now you're just gone."

His eyes go wide, and he runs both hands through his blond hair, frustrated. Sobriety nudges at my thoughts, making me aware of my surroundings. I'm on his doorstep, shouting about giving sexual favors for drugs, in his neighborhood. Oh, fuck. What am I doing?

Making an idiot of myself, that's what I'm doing. "I'm sorry," I whisper. I race back to the cab without giving Evan another glance, slip inside, slam the door, and urge the driver to *go*.

Shit. I didn't want him to know that side of me. I never wanted to share those things with him. Hell, even Andee doesn't know the depths to which I sunk when I was locked in the clutches of addiction. I thought Evan and I were beyond repair, before. Now I'll be lucky if he can look at me again without pity or disgust in his eyes. I let myself into my apartment, lock it behind myself.

I'm alone. No Andee. No Evan. Even The Core isn't mine anymore, and The Haven is so big... so empty and full of unknowns. My heart sprints. I stagger to the bathroom and stare at my reflection in the mirror. Everything behind me is shifting, swirling, and I look like a nightmare.

This is what I am. Alone, spinning out of control, and ruining the lives of everyone around me. Evan must be so embarrassed by my behavior. And what if his dad was there? He'll have to explain it all to him... Oh, no. If he didn't hate me before, he sure does now.

I can't face him again. And I can't go back to The Core. Andee's the head of the place I've called home for so long. How the hell am I going to run a club on my own? I'm not cut out for this. I'm a goddamn whore, and I'll never be anything else. My own mother knew it, and they say your mother knows you better than anyone.

You'll never clean yourself up, she'd said to me when I picked up my belongings off her front lawn before she moved away. *You'll never amount to anything. You're not my daughter.*

I knew she was right, even as I begged her to reconsider. Since then, I've just been bandaging my wounds with this false sense of security at The Core. Convincing myself I'm something I'm not, lying to everyone and pretending I'm a decent human being. In reality, all I am is trash. I just fucking proved it. Tears spill down my cheeks, smearing dark streaks of mascara to my chin. I thread my fingers into my hair and pull until it hurts.

And then everything hurts. My heart—which was held together by the barest strings—implodes in my chest. Evan and I will never be what I'd just started to imagine we could become. Andee is too good of a person... I don't deserve her. She's going to college, and she's going to be successful. Derek is wrapping his business... his *investments*... around the lie that I'm better than I used to be. That he can trust me, that I'm *healed.* I can't let him do that. I'll only let him down like I do to everyone.

What a fucking joke I am. I laugh at myself scornfully in the mirror. I'm going to let them all down.

The corner of the Ziploc bag sticks out of my purse. I fish it out and rip it open. Start popping off lids and seeing what's inside. If I ever want to be the person everyone seems to think I am, I can't keep bits and pieces of this girl around anymore, locked in a drawer.

I line them all up on the counter. Twenty-one pills. I could just take them. Tip my head back and drop them in my mouth. Swallow them all dry, cup a handful of water from the faucet, and wash them down. It'll only take a few minutes for the novocaine to sweep through my bloodstream. Mixed with the booze, I'm sure to have a good, long sleep, and wake up without everyone's expectations bearing down on me. And then everyone will see what I am. They'll know better than to count on me for anything. I won't destroy Derek's investments or continue to feed Andee a lie she doesn't deserve. And Evan will see that I really am a monster. Not just a liar, not just a junkie, but a hopeless waste of air.

I sweep the pills into my hand. Tears spill down into my palm, wetting a few of the little, white tablets. One gulp of water, and this would all be over. Twenty-one is probably enough to kill me.

Something clicks in the apartment. The door? I stare at my palm. I'm out of time. If I'm going to do this, I've gotta do it now.

Five breaths go by, and still I'm staring at the pills. They're like little abusive lovers, these tablets. They tell me

154

they'll fix everything. I'll be fine, and I can keep them around and resist them. I don't need anyone else. I can do this all on my own, as long as I get that feeling... that rush... that the drugs promise me.

Andee pushes into the bathroom and stops dead in her tracks. Her eyes wander over the empty bottles of pills, and then her gaze settles on my hand and the twenty-one tablets I hold. She looks up at me, and her face drains to white.

"Is that all of them?" Her voice is barely above a whisper.

I nod, and my heart sprints, fast and painful, pounding in my head. "Every last one."

She gulps, and comes to stand beside me. Picks up the empty pill bottles one at a time and drops them into the trash. "What are you going to do?"

I stare at her for a long moment. She's giving me the choice. She's giving me her trust. Tears escape from my eyes again. I don't deserve her trust or this choice. But maybe... just maybe... I still have a chance to earn it.

I don't give myself a moment to change my mind. I turn to the toilet and drop all the pills into the water. They splash like raindrops, and a pang of loss hits me. I won't have these old lovers, anymore. If the going gets tough, I don't have a backup plan. I've lost Evan, and now I'm giving up my fallback, too. I flush the toilet. The water spins the tablets down into the sewer. My vision blurs with tears, and then I can't stay on my feet any longer.

"I need you, Andee," I sob.

I'm not sure how I get to the bedroom, but I know she doesn't leave my side all night.

Stand Tall

Andee refills my coffee and brings it to me on the couch. We're both in pajamas, snuggled up under a blanket with the TV on low in the background. She leans her head on my shoulder. "Pills and alcohol, Alice. What were you thinking? You scared me. When I saw all those empty bottles..."

I press my cheek to her hair, remorse nagging at my heart. "I know. I'm so sorry. I just got stuck in my head, you know? After seeing Evan tonight..."

"You saw Evan?" She lifts her head and peers at me with surprise. "Again?"

A groan of humiliation escapes me. "I went to his house when I left The Core."

"Oh, Alice, the only thing worse than drunk texting your ex is making a drunken appearance at his house."

"I know, I know. And I realized that. I just got thinking how badly I've led him on, and the pills seemed like the best answer."

"Where did you even get them all?"

"I've had them in my drawer at The Core since I got clean."

Her jaw falls open. "Why the hell would you keep them all this time?"

"I just thought if I kept them around and resisted them, I would be stronger for it, you know? I realize now that's stupid."

"Very stupid. You can't keep them around, Alice. You'll get trapped."

"I know."

We sip coffee in silence for a while. Someone raps quietly on the door, and Andee answers it. My toes freeze when I hear his voice.

"Is she alright?" Evan asks Andee.

"Yeah, she's okay," Andee says.

Silence follows for an agonizing moment, and then he speaks again. "Does she want to see me?"

Andee peers back at me, and I shake my head. I can't face him yet. I need to screw my head back on, first.

Andee tells him gently no.

"Okay," Evan says, and I feel a sharp pang in my heart at the disappointment in his tone. "Well, just tell her... if she needs me, she can come find me. I'm here."

"Thanks, Evan," Andee says. "I will."

Part of me wants to leap off the couch, throw open the door, and let him fold me into his arms forever. Part of me wants to cry against his chest and apologize for being such a bitch. The other part of me—a much bigger part—knows that I've gotta get myself together before I can see him again. I'm so ashamed of my behavior, and I can't go running off to Evan until I've figured out how the hell I ended up here. So I wait until Andee closes the door, grab my phone, and text Evan a simple, *I'm sorry.*

Only a minute passes and his reply comes: *Me too.*

"What can I do?" Andee asks as she sits down beside me once more. "How can I help you get through this?"

I could ask her to start random purse checks to keep me accountable to sobriety. I could ask her to check me in somewhere, or to let me score just *one* pill to get it out of my system. But I'm the one who needs to fix this. It isn't her problem, and it isn't something anyone can do but me.

"Just keep being the person I wish I was," I tell her.

She laughs, and leans on my shoulder again. "Ditto, Alice."

Throwing myself into work is the best way I can think of to recover from such an epic fall off the wagon. I get busy. Really busy. I dress my finest each day, handle meetings with grace, and eventually, The Haven starts to come together. Andee helps me enroll in a business management course at the community college. I know I can't handle the full immersion of University life, and I have too many responsibilities to do that, anyway. But I have wanted to go back to school for so long, and if I don't do it now, who knows? In another six months I might have convinced myself I can't. Two classes a week plus a few hours of study keeps my mind off my loneliness.

And the withdrawals. I had no idea one little slip of my sobriety could land me craving the pills so damn hard. I find myself staring at the medicine cabinet, reading the ibuprofen bottle, and wishing I could just take a handful or two. Somehow, I manage to resist, but it's sheer willpower.

I also start seeing a sobriety counselor in a group meeting once a week. My anger with Derek doesn't last long. It's not his fault I never finished dealing with my issues. I wanted to do this on my own, and I've done a decent job until now, but life just gets more complicated the older I get, and I know I need to develop some coping skills. I take Derek up on the offer to pay for my counseling, even though he seems a little surprised that we are on speaking terms at all.

My counselor's name is Mindy. She's a short, pixie-like woman who wears something with a butterfly on it every single day, whether it's her shirt, her scarf, or even on the heels of her shoes. I like her immediately. She's easy to talk to, and no matter what I tell her, she never acts surprised or repulsed as I start sorting out all of the bullshit in my past. She doesn't judge me, but she does tell me I need to really watch my drinking. It's a gateway to letting substances solve my problems, and I know she's right. She also tells me in private that she and her husband heard of The Haven, and are going to drop in sometime after the grand opening. Surprised as I am by it, it brings me a little sensation of pride that maybe I can help her in some way, too.

At night, my bed is cold. Too big without Evan wrapped up in the blankets. I wonder if he sleeps well without me. I sure as hell don't sleep well without him. But part of what I'm learning from my sessions with Mindy is that I have to be okay on my own without letting my thoughts run away with me. I can't fill every spare moment with The Core, dancing, drinking, socializing. I have to be able to have down time without stewing on my mistakes of the past, and without resorting to those old, comforting thoughts of numbness and pills. So I go to bed early some nights. I read books. I study. Sometimes, I'm still awake when Andee comes in late from The Core, and I end up back in the kitchen with her talking about nothing important, or about things that are very important. She doesn't push me, and I find myself thanking her probably more often than is normal simply for being my friend.

The bright, fluorescent lights blacken as I flip off the switch in The Haven. This is it: opening night. I've been working my ass off for the last three months, and I'm ready. The doors open in two hours, so it's my last chance to check that everything works right.

"Okay, hit it, Xander!" I call to the DJ. He doesn't hesitate. The neon lights come on, along with the black lights, which illuminate all the brilliant, white tables to the point of glow. I grin with excitement. I sure as hell picked the right colors for this place. Huge, long, abstract paintings of couples twisted into sexual positions line the walls above the booths and tables, and just like The Core, The Haven has three levels: an executive upper floor, and a rooftop. The dark red leather sofas look romantic under the club lights, and the go-go dancers start to make their way up to their cages with the help of the security staff. Despite my best efforts, I haven't found a decent matchmaker yet for the place, so I'll fill in that position myself until the right person comes along. It really is a job that requires unique skill sets.

The go-go cages are a little different here than in The Core. They're big enough for a few dancers at once, so I pair up two male dancers, two female dancers, a male/female couple, and I even have a ménage in one cage for opening night. Xander hits the music, and they start dancing together, looking sexy as hell in various outfits: formal dresses, bondage gear, and club wear. I decided on this arrangement of couples because I don't want anyone walking in and snubbing someone else for the interactions they see happening around them. I want it crystal clear when patrons walk in that this place is for open, free, loving minds only. Closed-minded assholes are not welcome.

The dancers are more explicit than a sign, I hope.

"Alice," the bartender calls, "problem."

I wave at Xander with approval, and he kills the music. The dancers cheer that everything is ready to go for opening night, and then they climb down to relax until the crowd starts flooding in. We've had quite a bit of publicity lately, so I expect it will be a busy night.

But of course it's not going to go off without a hitch. The bartender's having an issue with the CO_2. I can't seem to fix it, and nobody likes flat, non-carbonated pop, so I tell Xander to hold down the fort while I run over to The Core to grab an extra tank. I slip into my Escalade and make my way over there, drumming my hand impatiently on the steering wheel when I get stuck at a red light.

I pull up onto the curb beside the door to The Core, and my heart skids to a halt. Evan's bike is parked right behind Derek's truck, and the two guys lean against the big black beast, conversing casually. My heartbeat finally resumes, breaking into a sprint, and I take a few deep breaths to calm down before I hop out of the SUV.

"Hey Alice," Derek says. We've been on okay terms since the fight, but our relationship is more business-like than before. I know he's happy I'm in therapy, but I have to make my boundaries clear with him. He can't try to control what I do and don't do in my spare time.

"Hey," I say. "You two managed to kiss and make up?" I flinch as soon as it's out of my mouth, but Evan only chuckles.

"I think we'll skip the kissing part, if that's okay with you."

I give him a weak smile, and he pierces me with those green eyes. God, how can he still stop me in my tracks like this? Will I always feel this way when I see him: overwhelmed, and sorry that I lost him?

"You only got a couple hours," Derek says, checking his watch. "Everything okay?"

"Yeah, we're all set." I try to squash the tremor in my voice. "Um, except I need a new CO_2 if you have it. Something's wrong with ours."

"Sure, I'll grab you one." Derek pushes off his truck. "Be sure to let the liquor guy know when he comes by next. They have to reimburse you for it."

"Thanks, I will."

Derek gives me a smile and a wink. He disappears into The Core.

I dig my toe nervously into the ground, poking at a little dent in the concrete.

"Are you all ready for tonight?" Evan asks. "I didn't even realize The Haven was opening already."

"Yeah, time flies," I say. I can't meet his eyes. It brings up too much emotion, too much failure. *Deep, slow breaths, Alice.*

I see his feet in my field of vision before I notice he's crossed the sidewalk to stand right in front of me. That familiar smell hits me like a punch in the gut: his leather jacket, his cologne, his personal scent. I peer up at him, and his fingers find mine.

"Congratulations," he says. "I'm really proud of you."

His words dredge up a bunch of emotion, and I have to look away from him to keep it at bay. I let him hold my hand, though, and squeeze my eyes closed as his thumb runs back and forth across my knuckles.

"I never, ever meant to hurt you, Alice."

"I know." It's all I can manage, even though so many other things—important things—sit right on the tip of my tongue. I don't know how to get my voice around this lump in my throat.

"Can we talk? About us?"

I look up at him, surprised. "Is there still an *us*?"

Hope sparks in his gaze, but he swallows hard and doesn't answer that. I don't think he knows the answer any better than I do.

"I can pick you up tonight after work, if you want," he says. "You can tell me all about The Haven. I've been dying to hear your voice."

My heart stutters, and I breathe slowly again, overwhelmed. How I've missed him.

"Sure," I say. "But I won't be done until at least four in the morning."

"Then I'll see you at four."

162

The Core doors swing open, and Evan lets go of me before Derek sees us.

"Are you going to come by later?" I ask Derek.

"Yeah, I'll come in when it starts to get crazy. Help you close the night up." My boss loads the CO_2 tank into the back of the Escalade, and gives Evan a handshake.

"Bring your truck into Meyer's on Friday?" Evan asks. "I can have that leaky exhaust fixed by afternoon if you get it to me early."

"Sounds good," Derek says. Wow, they really have kissed and made up. I have to hide my giggle as I think it.

"Thanks, Derek," I say, making my way around to the driver's door of my SUV. "See you later, Evan."

"I'll pick you up," Evan replies with a grin. He shoots Derek a challenging glare, as if daring him to object. Derek just waves me on my way.

Whew. Not that I needed drama on my first night running The Haven, but oddly, the adrenaline spike from the encounter kicks my mood into a higher gear. I crank up the music and dance along as I drive, not giving a shit who's watching me. I'm opening my own sex club tonight. I'm clean, sober, and confident. I'm in school again. Derek and Andee support everything I do, and tonight, I get to see Evan. Even though we've broken up, I still don't want to leave things for good on the sour note we left them before.

The lineup is halfway down the block by the time I swing open the doors and invite all the couples inside The Haven. Xander is a demon on the tables, spinning music so energetic that even the most nervous new patrons break into dancing. Within minutes, the place is packed, and I even catch a glimpse of a reporter snapping a photo when I'm standing in the doorway. Good thing I look smoking hot in my nearly-bikini skirt and totally-bikini top, with that fur-edged jacket

Evan said he wanted to peel off me the night of Derek's party. I wonder what website he writes for.

The night flies off without a single speed bump. I hardly notice the hours go by, I'm so busy. A few couples hook up, but most of them come to acclimate, to watch. The place is on fire, illuminated by the best lights, and the liquor flows like water. By the time I guide the last couple to a cab on the street, the go-go dancers have climbed down, and they hug-tackle me to the floor. The night was a roaring success. I did it.

My Antidote

Evan's motorcycle rips up beside The Haven when I'm the only one left here. Everything's locked up and shut down. I slip my helmet over my head and climb astride the seat, my legs on either side of his hips.

"You still have your insurance policy," Evan says.

"Never left my backseat."

He chuckles, pushes the bike upright, and blasts forward. It's such a familiar comfort, clinging to Evan's back like this as he rides. I've missed this. I've missed him, so very much.

"Where to?" Evan calls over his shoulder.

Andee's probably already at my apartment. "Coffee shop or your house... your choice."

He tosses a sneaky grin back at me. "Still got that fearless streak, huh?"

"Should I be afraid?"

He shrugs. "Depends. If we go to my house, I can't promise I won't shred that outfit off your body."

Arousal hits me, hot and unrestrained, like a tsunami. "I guess we're going to your house, then."

Evan pushes the bike faster. Is this a good idea? I have no clue. Will falling back into Evan's arms negate all the progress I've made, all the growing I've done? Evan's seductive intensity is so hard to resist. I have to make sure I don't lose sight of my own needs if I turn my focus back onto him. Onto *us*.

He parks in the driveway and leads me inside by the hand. I glance around the entryway and find no sign of his dad's shoes. "Are we alone?"

Evan peels off his leather jacket and hangs it up. "Yeah. Dad's been staying at home more often. He and I kind of had a disagreement, but we're cool now."

"About what?" My mouth goes dry as I remember screaming at Evan on his doorstep. I hope I didn't cause a rift between them.

"About me needing some space." He takes my hand again and leads me to the kitchen. Coffee's already on, and I toss him a smirk. He must have known I'd choose to come here.

I sip my coffee tentatively as Evan sits across from me at the little, round glass table. It's a heavy silence, and I know there's so much I need to say, but again, I can't seem to spit it out.

"How the hell did things go so wrong with us?" Evan says, breaking the quiet. His fingers stroke across my palm, and the touch wakes up sensations inside me I haven't felt since before I realized how deep the addiction's claws were still hooked into my soul. "We were perfect together. You're everything I ever wanted, and I just threw it away at the first sign of trouble. I'm sorry."

"It was kind of a big sign," I say. "Not many guys would want to stay with a girl after all the things I told you."

Evan's expression twists into anger in a heartbeat. "That's what you think happened? That we broke up because you've got some shit in your past?"

"It's a lot of shit. It's *bad* shit." My mind automatically starts listing all the ways I've fucked up, but I shake it off. I can't get stuck in those thoughts.

"You're dealing with it though, aren't you? Derek says you've been in therapy."

"Derek needs to learn to keep his fucking mouth shut about my business," I snap.

Evan sighs, pushing his coffee cup away from himself. "My point is that it doesn't define you. I don't think of you as the drunk girl shouting at me on my doorstep, Alice. I think of you as the fearless, powerful, untouchable woman who took my breath away the first time I saw her."

My heart rocks with love at his words. It's too potent, and the wounds still bleed so easily. "Please don't," I whisper.

"No, listen to me. I can't stand the thought of you hurting. The shit in your past... I don't care. It all shaped you into this beautiful woman I adore. I love every single thing about you. Even the dark things."

He leans forward, touches my chin with his fingertip, and wordlessly begs me to look at him. "I love you, Alice. I've been miserable without you. You deserve to know how I feel about you."

"Please." A tear makes its way out of my eye, and I dash it away.

"Why, baby?" Evan says. "Why can't you let me love you just as you are?"

I can't slow my shaking. Everything he says brings up passion that's too powerful for me to resist. "I've never stopped loving you, Evan. But it hurts too much to think about losing you again, and I can't promise I won't disappoint you."

He's quiet for a long moment.

"I killed my brother, Alice."

I open my mouth to object, but he holds up a hand, begging me to listen.

"You may not see it that way. My dad may not see it that way. The judge, even my grief counselor, they don't see it that way—yeah, I'm in therapy too... that was part of my fight with Dad—but I see it that way. And I guess I don't know how to let *you* love *me*." He lets out a mirthless laugh. "Hell, I don't even know how you *can* love me. But that's my problem, not yours. I'm working through it. I can't promise I won't disappoint you, either. I can only promise you one thing: if you'll stick by me and be patient with me while I'm trying to move on from all the bullshit, I'll do the same for you."

I stare at him as he opens a window into his soul for me to see through. Every time he's done it before, I've slammed the door to my own heart in his face. Not this time. He deserves better from me.

"I want to be yours, Evan," I say. "I want to show you all the sides of me you're willing to see... from the bad days to the good days and every moment in between."

Relief washes over Evan's face. He chuckles. "We're both so fucked up. At least we're fucked up together. I don't want another minute without you."

His words steal my breath and throw it far away from my reach.

"This is not how I planned I would do this," he says.

"How did you plan it?"

He licks his lips, and then he leans forward, cups my chin, and pulls me across the table for a kiss. It's slow, at first... exploratory. But I welcome his hesitant tongue when he tastes me, and his eyebrows knit together with the struggle to restrain himself. When he releases me, his eyes smolder with desire.

"That's kind of how I hoped this would go," he says in a husky voice loaded with need.

I touch my lower lip with my thumb. God, how I've missed his kiss.

"May I show you something?" Evan asks.

I don't have words. I just nod, my skin flushed with desire.

He takes my hand and pulls me to a little door off the hallway behind the kitchen. It leads to the garage, and he flicks on the light before leading me inside.

The light is dim, but before me stands a motorcycle. It's sleek, much different from Evan's bike, but the airbrush design—blue flames and dice—is all scratched up. And most of the parts look twisted or bent. Then it dawns on me. This is one of the matching bikes in the picture in his room, when he sat beside Mickey.

"I've been trying to fix it up as best I can," Evan says. "I don't know what the hell I'm going to do with it. Dad says I should scrap it, but I just can't bring myself to."

"Is it yours?" I ask, meeting his eyes. They're dark and severe. "Or Mickey's?"

He grimaces. "There wasn't enough left of Mickey's to keep. Dad didn't ask for it when it happened, and I was still sedated so I couldn't do anything about it."

I run my hand along the damaged gas tank. "You did the artwork?"

He nods. "I always loved the idea of dice. Taking a chance, risking it all to score big, or lose everything at once."

I meet his eyes. "Is that what tonight is? Rolling the dice?"

He cracks half a grin that doesn't touch his eyes. He takes my chin in his fingertips and tilts me up. "You're worth risking everything."

When his lips touch mine, tears prick behind my eyes. I can taste his care for me in the kiss... even after everything we've been through, he's still so afraid of losing me.

"How did you envision this?" Evan asks. "Our reunion."

I don't have thoughts to form into words. When Evan kisses me, it all evaporates... all the worries, all my insecurities. It's what I crave from him. What I need. I tangle my fingers into his hair and kiss him hard. He groans against my lips.

His hands slide around my waist, and he lifts me up. Carries me, wrapped around him, all the way up the stairs to his bedroom. He lays me down in the darkness and I hear the rustle of his jeans as he peels them off, and then his smooth, hard body presses along mine. Every inch of him is warm, and I writhe as he kisses me again, his tongue slipping in and out of my mouth every time. He works my skirt off slowly, but loses his patience to get me naked. The bikini top doesn't survive the intensity of his groping hands. He tears it away from my breasts, revealing all of me to him, and I can't slow my hands in his hair, along his shoulders, and across his scarred back.

Do I really get to still have this with him? I almost fear I'm dreaming.

He tortures me for the longest time, poised at my entrance but not willing to deliver himself into me just yet. He kisses me until I'm whimpering with need, and then pulls back to peer into my eyes under the dim light of the rising sun.

"I love you, Alice," he murmurs. "Don't let me be that stupid again. Don't ever let me lose you."

I open my mouth to soothe him, but he jams himself forward, filling me in one smooth, hard stroke. I cry out at the sudden fullness. Evan worships my neck with his mouth, and within moments, I'm lost to his pleasure. He moves in slow, deliberate strokes, thickening inside me. I dig my fingertips into his biceps at the delicious anticipation, needing more of him inside me. His hands graze my breasts, my hips, my cheeks. He touches me like he's never touched me before, like this is our first time and there is so much to learn about one another.

And then he picks up his pace, and I arch up against him. His weight presses down on me, trapping me to his bed in the best way possible, and my pleasure builds with each thrust. His breath is harsh and rapid against my cheek, and he grasps my chin with his fingertips, turning me so I have no choice but to take his kisses. I welcome each one eagerly, tightening inside, and he pulls away to watch me as I near the edge of oblivion.

"Give it to me, Alice," Evan begs. "Give me everything."

I do. I let go, my orgasm rippling up from my toes and slamming back through my body, clenching him inside me so tight he calls out at the sensation. And then he buries himself all the way in the deepest part of my body and stills, losing himself in my warmth. He collapses against me, shaking hard, and I wrap around him in every way I can.

This feeling is better than any high. The pleasure of a handful of pills doesn't even come close to touching this pinnacle. His body fills mine and his words fill my heart. Irresistible, relentless Evan. He's all I've wanted for so long.

"I never want to let you go," Evan whispers as we coast down from the aftershocks of mutual orgasm.

"Then don't," I say. I wouldn't let him if he tried.

We may have been beaten into submission by the demons that haunt our nightmares, but we're not broken anymore. Picking up the pieces of ourselves—of each other—and fitting them together might not be an easy task.

Lucky for me, he's not the type to turn his back on a challenge. And neither am I. We are stronger when we're with each other. We'll fight to be better together than we've ever been alone. One day—one kiss—at a time.

A Message From The Authors:

If you or someone you know is battling addiction, please seek help. Prescription medication can be as damaging—and as daunting—as any other substance. Don't hesitate to tell someone if you need help.

If you're grieving or in pain, reach out to those around you. You are not alone.

Thank you so much to everyone who has supported us in the journey that is The Core! First and foremost, readers, we owe you everything. Thank you so much for reading and sharing our stories with others. You're more important to us than coffee. We love you. LOVE.

Thank you to our families, friends, and fellow authors as always for being so supportive of what we do.

Thank you to Enticing Journey Promotions for the AMAZING blog tour. You make us feel so unbelievable loved, and we are so grateful for everything you do.

Thank you to Michelle Johnson of Inklings Literary Agency for supporting all our projects, and for teaching us to "80's dance" in New Orleans when we were tearing up the dance floor to Firework.

Stalk The Authors...

Check out the first series in THE CORE: Andee – IGNITE is free on most venues, and the box set is available in paperback and ebook!

Twitter: @NolaSarina, FB: Author Nola Sarina

Twitter: @EmilyFaith2012, FB: Author Emily Faith

And join the email contact list for regular updates, or be a part of our Pimp Crew...
http://www.nolasarina.com/contact/

For dark, sexy, paranormal fun, check out *Wild Hyacinthe* by Nola Sarina & Emily Faith

Also watch for Nola Sarina's dark fantasy VESPER titles.

If you join our Pimp Crew, you'll have access to advance cover reveals, news about releases and appearances, exclusive excerpts and have the chance to land Advance Reader Copies of our books! Just stalk one of us down and drop us a note letting us know you're in. We love our Pimps!

Proof

Made in the USA
Charleston, SC
08 October 2014